Iain Levison was born in Aberdeen, Scotland, in 1963. Since moving to the US, he has worked as a fisherman, carpenter and cook, and detailed his woes of wage slavery in *A Working Stiff's Manifesto*. He currently lives in Raleigh, North Carolina.

DOG EATS DOG

Iain Levison

BITTER LEMON PRESS
LONDON

BITTER LEMON PRESS

First published in the United Kingdom in 2008 by
Bitter Lemon Press, 37 Arundel Gardens, London W11 2LW

www.bitterlemonpress.com

First published in French as *Une canaille et demie* by
Éditions Liana Levi, Paris, 2006

A CIP record for this book is available from the
British Library

ISBN 978–1–904738–31–2

Typeset by Alma Books Ltd
Printed and bound in Great Britain by Cox & Wyman Ltd,
Reading, Berkshire

Dog Eats Dog

1

Hitler was right.

Elias White scrawled the three words across a pad of paper, waiting for the students to arrive and for his 9:30 class to start. No, too provocative. *Hitler was right?* No. That made him sound unsure, something he tried never to be, neither in person nor in his writing. *Was Hitler Right?* It'd do, but it could be improved upon. He'd have to think about it.

Elias was trying to decide on a title for his newest article, a 15,000-word examination of Jewish issues in pre-war Germany, which he was nearly one hundred percent sure would be picked up by the Harvard *Historical Review*. He had already mailed it off, but had decided to change the title later. The title was everything. He wanted it to be shocking enough for the Harvard professors to notice and discuss it. He wanted the professors to be impressed by his courage in presenting an argument which flew so virulently in the face of political correctness. He imagined their faces as they read the title with horror; then, as they read on, they would be reassured by his intelligence, reason, and multi-colored graphs.

7

Elias also wanted the article to be posted on White Supremacist websites, so he could argue furiously against its misinterpretation by evil people with a harmful agenda. This kind of conflict usually resulted in the most prized of all commodities, news coverage. He imagined himself arguing his case on CNN, protesting with Chris Matthews, trading friendly jibes with Bill O'Reilly, perhaps even losing his temper and demolishing a token White Supremacist. The *Historical Review* was always looking for content of this sort, an opportunity to spark lively debate, and the name Elias White would soon be a perfect fit for their plans.

Elias White was a junior history professor who said what he thought, not what he was told to think. He was a man who presented arguments about Nazism, hate, power, and human nature, while others argued about who really invented the cotton gin. He was not afraid of hot-button topics. He was a researcher who traveled all over the world for his provocative and challenging articles. And he was going to get tenure.

The original premise of Elias's article was that the persecution of Jews in Nazi Germany was actually a symptom of class struggle, an explosion of resentment by working-class Germans against a segment of the population they perceived as middle-class or rich. White got the idea while on vacation in Germany with his girlfriend Ann, who was interviewing for a six-month post-doctoral study program at Heidelberg University. There, he had been wandering around the musty book stacks in the library, and – crouching down as if looking for some crucial document, while actually trying to get a peek up the skirt of a German girl studying at a desk – he stumbled across a box of handwritten journals.

The journals were the diaries of local German soldiers who had fought during the Second World War, collected by the university and translated into English by a German graduate student in 1955. While waiting for the girl to uncross her legs, White sat and browsed through the diary of an artillery officer captured on D-Day. His leg had been amputated – needlessly, the officer felt – by an American Jewish doctor. While recovering in England, the officer, Heinz Werthal, scripted a ten-page rant about how the Jews owned everything and could never be trusted. White knew he had struck academic gold.

The diaries were in a box marked "Mull", which, White remembered from three years of high-school German, meant "trash". There were three other boxes there, full of diaries, documents and writings. They were from soldiers, housewives and even a few leading German intellectuals, all ready to go out the back door to the garbage pile, all full of Nazi rants. It was beautiful.

Especially good was that they were on the way to the trash. It gave White the opportunity to claim that the documents were "rescued". In fact these documents were about to be "destroyed", which was almost as intriguing as being "banned". White already knew that his description of the discovery of the diaries would contain a passage about how he had searched for them for many years. It wasn't a lie. He was always looking for cool documents to write journal articles about. Following the German girl into the library had nothing to do with it.

"You have to be careful about seeming to present Nazism as a positive force," Ann had written back from Heidelberg after Elias had returned home and sent her the first draft.

Ann had missed the whole point. There was something about academia she just didn't get. It was going to hurt her significantly throughout her career, Elias knew. She was always *studying*. Learning and knowledge had very little to do with it, once you had mastered the basics. Once you had studied enough so that you could find Poland on a map and you knew the names of the last three Presidents, the rest was mostly opinion. It was all in how confidently you expressed yourself. He had tried to bring her up to speed on this a few times, and arguments always resulted. And the trick wasn't to be the smartest person in the room. That stopped being important in third grade. The trick was getting yourself noticed.

Students began to trickle into the room. Elias looked down at the paper he had been doodling on, and saw three letters he had penned in majestic, swirling script underneath his name: HAR. The rest, VARD PROFESSOR, would have to come later. He had a class to teach.

"Most of humanity," Chico said, "isn't worth the bullets it would cost to kill them."

Think of the implications of that comment, Dixon thought. Unlike the rest of them, Dixon's time in prison had not been wasted, because he had learned to think of the implications of other people's comments. He had learned to think about all kinds of things. He had spent nine years looking out windows, staring at the prison laundry, at the workout yards, watching, learning, about humanity. The others were thinking about the best way to get a free carton of smokes and he was thinking about karma, and souls, and the significance of actions and the meaning of life. Dixon had not come to any firm conclusions, wasn't sure there were any, but he had learned to think.

For instance, before Chico uttered his comment, Dixon had been wondering about how badly it damaged your karma to point a shotgun in a teller's face and get them to give you the bank's money. Not as badly as pulling the trigger, he had decided. Pointing the gun and scaring the shit out of someone was a forgivable act, one you could make up for. You could give some of the money to a worthy cause and be done with it. You could use the money to end suffering, even if it was your own, and be karmically back to square one. The important thing was not to pull the trigger. So then, why load the gun? In case the cops showed up. Then you'd have to kill a cop. But that was a different issue, because they were armed and could kill you. Self defence.

The debate could go on and on.

But Dixon realized, from Chico's one comment, that he was in a lot of trouble. These other three had no sense of karma. He sensed that they didn't really want to rob the bank. What they wanted was to wield The Power, that ultimate power you have when you pull out the shotgun and wave it around and people respond. Boy, do they ever respond. They'll lie down when you tell them, they'll roll over, they'll bark like a dog if you like. You've got five or six people, bank managers, housewives, bosses of small firms, anyone who happens to be in the bank at the time, who'll do whatever you say. If The Power is the point, then the chances that the bank will be robbed successfully are slim. The other three are going to drag out The Power, make it last longer than necessary, Dixon knew. And time meant cops. And cops meant a shootout. And a shootout meant everyone going out in a blaze of glory and no money and no farmland outside Edmonton, Alberta, which had been his plan all along.

It was too late to back out now. They were on their way to the bank.

Dixon had a bad self-image, but his image of humanity in general was even worse. He thought he was lower than snake shit – and he was one of the noblest people he knew. These other three in the back of the van had not a single positive characteristic he could think of that would make him feel anything if they were to be shot dead.

They were not dumb people, Dixon knew. Chico was smart, aggressive and charismatic, and had organized this whole robbery from scratch. Without Chico, Dixon might well be working in the lumberyard for the rest of his life, six dollars an hour and a rooming house and three visits a week to his parole officer. His first two months out, he had no energy to do anything, just took himself back and forth from work, and crawled into his bed in his tiny room and looked at the ceiling until it was time to go to work again. He didn't wish he were back in prison, but he did occasionally wish he were dead. There was no reason to go on, nothing to look forward to but a life of punching in, punching out. Sleep wake work sleep. He mentioned his depression to the court-mandated counsellor, who was not interested.

The court-mandated counsellor had been counseling cons for fifteen years and figured if they mentioned depression they were trying to score a prescription for pills so they could sell them on the street. The court-mandated counsellor was interested in whether Dixon was using illegal drugs. The counsellor shrugged, said "It's normal" and tested his piss.

Then Chico came along, a machine operator at the lumberyard, and began talking about the bank. Chico was the type of person Dixon no longer wanted to know, a criminal who believed crime was his calling, with a hatred for the straight and narrow and a professed feeling of brotherhood for all cons. Chico ranked people according to the seriousness of their crimes. Dixon's multiple armed robbery convictions put him just below a murderer, high praise indeed from a sociopath like Chico, and necessary experience for the job he was planning.

At first Dixon had been hesitant. He really did consider parole a second chance, and there was a part of him that wanted to be a normal civilian, just a guy who had his own place and went to work and had a family. But he knew he was kidding himself. "Guys like us don't have families," Chico told him. "Not until we make the big score. Then we have a family and live in a country with no extradition laws." Chico laughed. "American girls don't want the likes of you and me."

That sounded about right to Dixon. He was so convinced no women wanted to talk to him that he avoided the eyes of the pretty teenager who sold him coffee and a bagel every morning on his way to work, at the small store across from the bus stop. He never spoke to Lois, the leggy secretary at the lumberyard, and whenever there was paperwork to hand in to the office he would give it to one of the other guys, who would take it just for an opportunity to view her firm calves. Dixon didn't even entertain the idea of visiting a prostitute, which the other men in the rooming house told him was a rite of passage for parolees. Dixon considered himself not good enough for prostitutes. And yet he also considered himself to be one of the finest human beings in the prison system.

"Hey man," Chico asked Dixon as they both slumped against the wall in the back of the speeding van. "You look good all shaved up. You got a date later?"

Dixon had shaved the night before, shaved off a beard he had been growing for ten years, a beard that made him look like a member of a biker gang. It was a badge of working-class toughness, all the country boys in the Maximum Sec block had one, and Dixon had removed it without a word to anyone. Got a haircut, too. Now he hoped he looked like a businessman late for a plane. Chico wasn't paying him a compliment on his new, clean-shaven appearance, Dixon knew. Chico thought something was up.

"Dixon, how come you got a hammer and a chisel, man?"

He didn't sound suspicious, just curious. Guys often changed their appearances just before a robbery. The cops always showed an old photo of you. Dixon smiled his easy, winning smile, which he had learned to use to disarm people, and turned up the slow Southern drawl, magnifying the effect. "You don't ever know what you're gonna run into, pardner," he said.

Chico waved his sawn-off shotgun, making Dixon flinch. These guys knew less about gun safety than they did about bank robbery. "That's what these are for, man."

Dixon grinned at him. These men he was going to rob the bank with were not dumb, but dumb had nothing to do with it. The dumbest criminal Dixon had ever known, his cousin, once robbed a liquor store and got away with it. Mostly, he got away with it because Dixon got tried and convicted of the crime, due to his physical similarity to his cousin and because they both had the same name.

After the trial, family members made the cousin come forward and confess to the police that they had the wrong guy, but by this time Dixon had already been convicted, and the DA couldn't admit he'd just convicted the wrong guy. It was a five-year term, Dixon's first stint, and he did it as a juvenile offender as he was only sixteen at the time. By the time Dixon got out, just shy of his twenty-second birthday, he had become a hardened criminal. The cousin had got a job and straightened out his life.

Being smart had nothing to do with it.

What mattered was your karma, and these three looked karmically bankrupt. Where did that leave him? Maybe he was too and he just didn't realize it yet. If you judged a man by the company he kept, then Dixon was in trouble.

Which was nothing new.

Elias White's students loved him. He was one of the most popular teachers on campus. He was good looking, young (for a professor), charismatic and funny. He had a habit of failing no one who made even the slightest effort, and an unspoken yet widely known policy of boosting the grades of pretty girls who sat up front and wore skirts. It was ironic, therefore, that White hated teaching.

He couldn't stand it. It was a complete waste of his time. What he really wanted to be doing was research, writing, and going on talk shows. He wanted to elevate himself in the academic world, focusing on his specialty, which was Germany between the wars. He wanted to reach and go beyond the pinnacle that his father had reached fairly early on in his career, where his words were a marketable product, his seeming genius and originality acclaimed, his theories widely admired. At the young age of forty, his father had published a book on the Russian Revolution and three years later was a full Professor at Tiburn College. White wanted his own career to follow the same arc, but he didn't want to wait until he was forty – and Tiburn, where White now taught, was chicken feed.

Elias White's father had been a sly, political old rooster whose unremarkable intellect was complemented by a remarkable desire to avoid work. After graduating high school a year late, and getting fired from three jobs for excessive laziness, Cornelius White Jr had been the black sheep of a working-class Boston family who prided themselves on their ability to be inconspicuous. Rather than have the family name besmirched by a son who couldn't even achieve mediocrity, Cornelius White Sr pulled strings for his son to be drafted just as the Second World War was winding down. Convinced that a son who had died in the war made a better story than a son who was forever getting arrested for public drunkenness, Cornelius the Elder tried to arrange for his embarrassing namesake to see as much action as possible.

In this respect, the old man seriously misjudged his son's skill in avoiding anything unpleasant. Within weeks of being landed in war-torn Europe, Cornelius Jr had secured a job as a hospital orderly in liberated Paris. He did this by using his family-given superpower for blending into the background and getting lost in the confusion, so that his absence from any given assignment was never noticed. When a truckload of wounded soldiers stopped for water at his encampment outside the Huertgen Forest, White simply hopped aboard and wandered off for good, just as his unit was ordered to the Ardennes to be overrun in the Battle of the Bulge.

By the time the war ended in May of 1945, Cornelius White Jr had become a highly unnoticed member of a military hospital in Paris, soon to become an anonymous face in the crowd of soldiers sent to West Berlin. It was here that he found his calling. One day in the winter of 1946, he wandered off from his job at a marshaling yard unloading trains, and walked into an American-run schoolhouse for displaced German girls. From the vantage point of the empty but toasty-warm classroom, Cornelius White Jr looked through the filthy windows at his countrymen unloading trains and decided that he was going to become an educator.

It took only a few weeks of lying to priests, nuns and Army officers, and a forged document here and there, before White was admitted to an army school that trained teachers as part of the effort to rebuild post-war Germany. Over the next six years, while teaching, White tried to learn Russian, as he knew speakers of the language were soon to be a hot commodity. The task was beyond him. It seemed like the most complicated language in the world. His instructors and other students at the language institute would pull their hair out over his inability to grasp simple concepts of grammar. After six years, however, his smattering of Russian, combined with what he knew of Russian history simply from hanging out with the teachers, was enough to get him a teaching post at a small New Hampshire college when he was discharged in 1952.

In the world of academia, Cornelius White Jr had found the perfect place for his talents. His God-given ability to slither around unnoticed was rewarded each year with a fatter paycheck and a slimmer workload, until, after forty years of teaching, he found himself collecting nearly $100,000 for teaching one class a semester. But in 1992, an auditor finally did what so many others had failed to do. He noticed Cornelius White. But at that point, there was little to do but ask him to retire, which White did with a pension nearly half his salary and no workload at all.

The only other person to notice White was his wife, Janet, and she only briefly. Impressed more by his résumé than his personality, which was near non-existent, Janet

Korda was a secretary at Tiburn College whose goal in life was to marry either a war hero or a professor. Cornelius' battalion had been issued a unit citation after the Battle of the Bulge, and his ingratiating manner with the heads of the college was all but guaranteeing him a professorship, meaning that Janet could kill two birds with one stone. By the time she began to suspect that Cornelius had never seen combat and was a dunce, she had a twelve-year-old son, Elias, the result of two weeks' worth of sexual abandon at the beginning of the marriage. She carried on with her loveless and sexless marriage until one day deciding she wanted to become an actress, at which point she set off for Hollywood without warning or discussion. A letter was left on the table, which Elias found one afternoon on his return home from junior high school. The Whites never heard from her until the LAPD mailed her personal effects back home a year later, with a newspaper article about a hotel room slaying.

It was at his father's funeral in 1995 that Elias White looked around and decided to make some changes in his family history. The event was attended by hundreds of people from Tiburn, a tribute to the remarkable power of familiarity, to the warm feelings that people have for the predictable and uninteresting. It occurred to none of these people, Elias knew, that in a lifetime of supposed accomplishment, his father had accomplished nothing but an act of sustained fraud on the entire world. And as they draped an American flag over his casket while a Vietnam veteran from the local VFW played Taps, as Cornelius White Jr's casket was dropped into the dirt where it belonged, Elias determined that come hell or high water, he was going to be noticed. The New Hampshire Whites were not going to shuffle past any longer. They were going to stride. He was going to make a mark on the world.

"Go! Go! Go!" Chico yelled as he slid open the side door of the van and leapt out. Dixon jumped out the back, followed by two Mexican kids waving shotguns like they were tennis rackets.

Immediately, Dixon knew they had a problem. The van had pulled up over thirty feet from the front door of the bank. Thirty feet! The two seconds it would take for masked men with rifles to run that distance to the door would be about one and three-quarter seconds longer than needed for a teller to hit a silent alarm, perhaps even an automatic door lock. The alarm would go off before the robbery even started. What the fuck were they thinking?

Chico walked into the bank and fired a twelve-gauge shotgun into the ceiling tile.

"Awright, you fuckers, listen up! We just want the money! Give us the money and no one gets hurt!"

There was silence. There always was. In the movies people screamed, but in real life, they just stood there, petrified, horrified by the idea that they might be noticed. They were deer in headlights. Ceiling dust and gun smoke wafted around the room.

Chico was shouting instructions about staying on the floor and Dixon could hear him as he pushed against the teller's door leading behind the counter. It was open. It always was. The tellers never locked their own door, their final failsafe, except for a few weeks after a robbery. Then they got lax again. Dixon walked back behind the tellers, who were standing at attention while one of Chico's Mexicans ran in behind him and began looting their drawers. He was even taking the coins.

He was taking the coins. That was what happened when you robbed a bank with maniacs. It was impossible to find a good partner these days. The Mexican was pointing a pistol in the face of the teller, enjoying her terror. "Get on the floor," he was shouting. She was already in a kneeling position.

In a small office with a window out to the tellers' station Dixon could see a manager standing, looking out, arms at his sides, helpless. Dixon pushed open the manager's door, looked out, closed it behind him.

"Where's the back door?" he asked, his pistol pointed at the manager.

"We . . . we don't have a back door."

"All buildings have more than one door. That's one, where's the other one?"

"You mean the employee entrance?"

"Hey now, do you think that's the fucking door I'm talking about? Where is it?"

The manager started to motion. "You take a right, out this door . . ."

"Show me, don't tell me. And if you move your hands away from your sides again you're a dead man."

"I . . . I . . . Don't shoot me!"

"SHUT THE FUCK UP!" Dixon watched him for the expected and immediate effect, of silence and complete obedience. It worked. It always did. "Show me where this door is."

Dixon could hear Chico intimidating the tellers and customers. His words had exactly the same lilt and manner as the block warden's spiel at Falstaff Correctional Center when the new inmates got the intro speech in that drone of unquestionable authority. "Any man caught masturbating in a public area will lose a point. Any man caught fighting will lose a point. Any man caught stealing food from the mess will lose a point. And believe me, you don't want to lose three points."

"Any one of you that slows us up will be shot," Chico was droning as he paced back and forth with the shotgun held high in one hand. "Any one of you that looks up or looks around will be shot." The lilt of his voice was a perfect impression of the block warden. Chico had The Power. *He* was the man in charge.

The bank manager was leading him to the back door, past the vault. Dixon grabbed the man's shirt.

"Wait here."

He positioned the bank manager directly outside the vault door and pulled the door open. It was unlocked. It always was. Look around, what do you see? Three trays piled high with hundreds. Dixon pulled a black laundry bag out of his pocket and with one smooth movement swept the stacks of hundreds into the bag. Dozens of them spilled onto the floor and he left them there, twisted the laundry bag shut. He turned to the bank manager. "Let's go."

The Mexicans were still pulling money out of the cash drawer and terrorizing the tellers. Dixon actually heard a handful of quarters spill onto the floor and, as he turned the corner with the bank manager, out of the corner of his eye he saw one of the guys scrambling for the coins. When were these guys ever planning to go for the vault? He had left plenty in there for them. Were they going to have coffee first?

The manager walked him down a carpeted hall, took a left, opened a door and there was a back door. A big, beautiful back door.

"That's alarmed," said the manager, pointing to the

door. "The second you open it an alarm will go off. It's real loud, too."

"Turn the alarm off."

"It's timed. If I try to turn it off before 11:30, it'll go off."

Dixon didn't have time to ask why. He took out his hammer and chisel and started whacking away at the alarm box. Sparks flew. The metal began to change shape, and he took the chisel, jammed it between the door and the box and jerked it halfway off the door. The alarm began to go off, a feeble gurgling. Dixon pushed the door open.

"Gimme your car keys."

They heard gunshots. The manager stiffened and turned pale. "What was that?"

"Cops are here. Gimme your car keys."

"Cops?" The man looked mystified, dazed. Dixon knew the trick. It was a delaying tactic, because he didn't want to give up his car keys. This man was trying to act dumb.

"Gimme your fucking car keys or your brains'll be all over the floor in three seconds. Three two . . ."

"Gaaaagh!" He was flipping backwards as if standing on an electric fence, body jerking, trying so hard to get the keys out of his pocket that he was almost going into convulsions. He pulled out a ring of keys. Dixon easily spotted the car key.

"What color is the car?"

"Blue. A blue Nissan Maxima."

The guy had balls. It was black, Dixon knew. He'd watched the manager getting into it every night for the last week. It was a black Nissan Maxima. He parked it in the same place every day, a few yards from the employee door. "Lie down on the floor and count to fifty."

The manager lay down cautiously amid all the broken metal while Dixon unzipped his coveralls and revealed his business suit, tie slightly crumpled. He pulled off his boots and tossed them in the corner of the stairwell. There were a few more gunshots. He heard the van pulling off, gunshots and screeching tires. The van. His ride. He was glad he hadn't depended on it. He pulled the bank manager's shoes off, nice black loafers, and slipped them on his own feet, and threw the coveralls next to the boots.

"See ya," he said to the manager.

"Bye," said the manager reflexively, another thing that always amazed Dixon. How unwilling people were, despite the circumstances, to drop formalities. Dixon hopped out the door, looked around the corner, and saw the manager's black Maxima there. He pressed the keyless entry, threw the bag of money into the passenger seat, fired up the car and drove back behind the Wendy's next door. He looked in the rear-view mirror as he drove across the strip-mall parking lot, and he saw three cop cars parked outside the bank. A fourth was just now going back behind the bank to the employee entrance. The white van was on its side at the other end of the parking lot, having crashed head-on with a fire hydrant, which was spraying a fountain of water up into the air. As he pulled out the parking lot exit into traffic, he turned the radio on to drown out the noise of gunshots. The first station he came to was country, just what he was looking for. He drove carefully and quietly, and he was listening to the Dixie Chicks' latest as he pulled out onto Northbound Route 26.

2

Elias saw Melissa Covington on his porch when he pulled into his driveway. Dammit. Probably locked herself out again, he figured. He had been looking forward to opening a bottle of wine and kicking back in front of the television, another hard week of work under his belt. Now he was going to have to entertain Melissa until one of her parents came home. Sometimes they didn't come home until eight or nine.

"Hey, Melissa," he called to her as he grabbed his briefcase from the back seat. "How're you?"

"Hi, Mr White," she called back. "I locked myself the fuck out again." She was sitting on his porch couch, and appeared to be filing her nails. A bright, pretty eleventh-grader with rosy cheeks and short blond hair, she appeared the quintessential fifties' prom queen, and Elias was always surprised by the filth that came out of her mouth.

"Doesn't your Mom ever say anything to you about you saying fuck all the time?" Elias asked as he opened the door. Melissa, uninvited, got up and followed him into the kitchen.

"I don't say 'fuck' in front of my Mom. I only say it in front of people I feel comfortable with."

"I'm flattered." He tossed his briefcase and keys on the kitchen table and looked at his mail. Electricity bill. Supermarket coupons. Something addressed to "single occupant", from a dating service. I'm single, Elias thought? Maybe the mailman knows something I don't. Nothing from Ann. Again.

"Fuck yeah, you should be." She walked by him and grabbed a glass out of his kitchen cabinet and poured herself a glass of water from his chilled bottle in the fridge. "Mind if I watch MTV?"

She leaned back against the wall while she said it, slowly sipping her water, looking at him over the top of the glass. With her other hand she was fidgeting with the tie on her loose blue lacrosse shorts. Suddenly irritated, she put the glass on the kitchen table and began to unlace the tie, as if she were going to undress. She played with the tie for a second longer, then huffed, and came over to Elias and stood right next to him, holding her shorts – which were slipping down – by the tie, revealing powder blue panties.

"Could you help me with this?" she asked.

"What's the problem," said Elias, professional and competent, pretending not to notice where his attention was being drawn. She brushed lightly up against him and she held open her shorts, giving him a clear view.

"I can't get them tight enough. It was bothering me all during lacrosse practice." She looked up at him, their faces only inches apart, and Elias could smell the fresh sweat on her. "Could you tie it?"

"Hmmmm," said Elias, suddenly at a loss for words. He had been looking in the cabinet, wondering which bottle of wine he should open, and had been caught off guard by Melissa's sudden flirtation. Was it flirtation, or did she just need her shorts tied? Who couldn't tie their own shorts, for God's sake? She had been over three or four times before, waiting for her parents to come home, but had always just sat watching TV. She had never really attempted conversation before, except for a few questions about Ann's whereabouts. Elias took the tie of her shorts and began to tie a bow quickly, hoping to disguise the sudden trembling of his fingers. The result was a joke, and unraveled almost as soon as he let go.

"The string's frayed," he said, as if his statement of the obvious would clear the problem up.

"Yeah, I know," Melissa said, with a clear ring of disappointment in his competence. She walked back over to the table, picked up her water, and walked out of the kitchen, throwing him a look of bored distraction as she entered the living room, which Elias knew was actually to see if he was watching her. He was.

31

He reached into the cabinet, and with fumbling hands pulled out the first bottle of wine he touched. A Chilean Pinot Noir "blend". What did blend mean, he wondered? That they just threw in any old grape from the vineyard, probably. Why had he bought this wine? He looked at the bottle for a clue. He was usually a savvy consumer at the Wineseller, not apt to try something Chilean. Then he saw the price label: $3.99. Discount rack. He remembered thinking that even if it was vinegar, it wouldn't be a bad buy. He uncorked it and poured it, and wondered what to do now. Stay in the kitchen? Read and re-read his mail? Go up to the bedroom and start reviewing the term paper outlines his students had handed in today? He grabbed an empty glass and went into the living room, sat down on the couch next to Melissa.

"Want a glass of wine?"

Now it was all about distance and time.

A bank robbery in which people had been shot would make a splash, but the splash would have a distance limit and a time limit. The robbery had occurred in a fairly small town in southern New Jersey thirty miles from Philadelphia. It might get coverage on the Philadelphia TV stations, but New York and Baltimore would never hear about it. So heading into Philly was out.

That left two options: the route south, over the New Jersey Turnpike Bridge into Delaware, or the route north to New York. Delaware was small and unpopulated and the bridge traffic was just too easy to watch. Besides, the ultimate plan was to end up in Quebec, Canada, via Fort Kent, Maine, so there was no point driving south. The plan was to get himself lost amid the confusion on one of the most heavily trafficked roads in the world, the New Jersey Turnpike heading into New York. The dangerous part was the first hour of driving through small southern New Jersey towns, where the robbery would be top priority. Once he was out amid the crush of northbound traffic, and the turnpike opened into twelve lanes, he would be home free.

Then there was time. In the small towns, the robbery would remain the focus of police attention for up to forty-eight hours. As he approached New York, this number would decrease dramatically. By the time he reached Rahway, they'd be dealing with overturned trailer trucks and robberies of their own, and he would be just a mention on a list of things the police had to deal with. And in New York City, he'd be a face in the crowd.

By now, forty-six minutes after the robbery, the shooting was over and the bank manager had talked to the police. He had given the specifics of his car, and an APB had been put out. Every cop on the road was looking for a black Maxima. This would last until something else happened. Dixon was hoping for something big, a warehouse fire or another robbery. Odds were against it, but you never knew. Sometimes dumb luck came to your rescue.

His mind was whirring, the residue of the adrenaline rush from the robbery still keeping him jittery, alert and elated. It was late Friday morning. Great time to get lost in the traffic. Roads were getting clogged. Good. No, great. Great. Drive the speed limit. Signal when you change lanes. Drive close to big trucks, they conceal you. Almost out of gas.

Shit.

Almost out of gas. The bastard hadn't filled his tank. He would have to STOP! In New Jersey. Where you couldn't fill your own tank. New Jersey law required letting an attendant pump your gas. And all he had was hundred-dollar bills. So he would have to stop, and interact with another human being, the two things you never wanted to do when on the run. Why couldn't the damned gas tank be full? He could just drive and drive, to New York City, to Connecticut, to Rhode Island, Canada. To the farm he was going to buy in Alberta. But now he had to pull over. If only the bank manager had stopped for gas this morning, then all Dixon's carefully made plans would actually work for once.

He checked himself in the mirror, to see if he looked normal, one of the crowd. He didn't. The suit helped, but there was something about him he would have noticed

34

right away. It was his expression: hard, unforgiving, as alert as an animal of prey. It was possible he looked like a businessman, but he was a businessman who seemed to be waiting for the person next to him to pull a shank out of a sock. Dixon tried to soften his expression, relax his face, *think* like a businessman. I'm just a guy on his way to a business meeting who needs some gas. The resulting facial contortion made him look like he'd just eaten a lemon.

He took a deep breath and pulled into the gas station, where a teenage kid was waiting by the pumps. A few drops of rain appeared on the windshield, and Dixon knew immediately what it meant. Rain was good. Rain caused accidents, gave the cops something else to do. He prayed for a massive downpour. The kid looked expectantly in the window as Dixon rolled the window down.

"Fill 'er up," Dixon said.

"What kind of gas you want?" The question took Dixon by surprise. What kinds were there?

"Unleaded," he said.

"Yeah, I know that," said the kid. "What octane?" Dixon didn't want this conversation. It had already gone on too long. Now he was noticed. Two or three words and you were fine, anonymous, forgotten, but twelve or fifteen and people would remember you. What the fuck was octane? Was this a jet? He hadn't bought gas for a car in fifteen years, had spent most of the time in one cell block or another. "You pick it," he said.

"There's a price difference," said the kid, warming to the topic. "A nice new car like this probably doesn't need . . ."

"The cheapest," said Dixon. If the fucking bank manager was ever going to get this car back, it wasn't going to be with a tank full of primo gasoline. Fuck that asshole. Blue Maxima, my ass. One word like that could have got Dixon killed. "Whatever the fuck you got."

He had blown it. People in business suits didn't talk like that. The kid had noticed something, too. He was a sharp kid, Dixon could tell, the type who noticed everything. He was only about seventeen or eighteen, but he could already tell some stories. He might have worn handcuffs, lived like an animal for a bit himself. He might have been a junkie. Maybe he still was. But he noticed things, and now he was noticing there was something not right about Dixon.

"I'll give you the standard," the kid said.

Now Dixon had to mention that all he had was hundred dollar bills and that he would need change. Could the kid make change? Dixon looked into the laundry bag to see if there were any twenties or fifties in there, and didn't see any. Just a big beautiful pile of stacked, fresh hundreds. He looked up, startled, to see the kid staring through the window.

"Sir, you have to open the door."

"The what?" He was going to say "fuck" again but controlled himself. "Why do I have to open the door?"

"The gas tank door. The little door. You should have a lever in there."

Jesus Christ, when did buying a fucking tank of gas become such a nightmare of decision-making and technology? In the old days you could just pull up at a gas station and fill up. Now you had to have a conversation about octane and levers. Almost panicked now, he looked around the car's interior for a gas-tank lever. The kid was pointing down.

"It should be down by the seat."

Dixon looked down and saw a little lever with a logo of a gas pump on it, and out of relief he pulled it so hard that it came off in his hand. Oh well. At least the kid didn't see that. He was already filling it up.

How much damage had been done? Obviously, the kid had figured that this wasn't Dixon's car, if he didn't know about the gas-tank lever. And it was a no-brainer that Dixon didn't belong in a business suit. But where could he go with that information? Perhaps Dixon was just a foul-mouthed businessman who had borrowed someone's car. Raindrops began to pelt down on the roof and windshield, and the kid stepped back under an awning while the tank filled automatically. The rain turned into a downpour. Beautiful. Soon he would be out of this damned gas station, away from this kid, cruising and listening to the radio and losing himself amid traffic and rush-hour city drivers. There would be car wrecks from here to Philly and New York City, plenty to keep the troopers busy. Cops didn't like to get out of their cars and snoop around in the rain, either. Easier just to sit in your cruiser and wait for crime to come to you. The loud drumming on the roof gave him a warm feeling of contentment, driving away the anxiety of the last two hours. He reached into his pocket and lit a cigarette, cracked the window slightly to let the smoke out. He blew a long stream of smoke out the cracked window.

The kid was gone.

There was a state trooper coming up on the side of the car with his gun drawn.

"Motherfucker!" Dixon shrieked. He started the car and he heard someone yelling as he slammed into drive. The car jerked forward and drove as if the parking brake were on, and in the instant it took him to figure out this was because the gas hose was still connected to the car, the back window exploded. They were shooting at him. The car broke free of the pump and Dixon careened across the gas station, with six feet of black gas hose trailing after him. He was about to head back out onto the highway when he saw a local cop car come up and block the entrance, and he slammed on the brakes.

Decision time. What to do. Two cops, one state trooper and one local. There would be more, but only two for now. He turned the Maxima so it faced the local cop car and slammed on the accelerator. The cop had just started to open the door, quickly closed it and dove over into the passenger seat as the Maxima screeched right up to it. Dixon slammed on the brakes a second before contact, and jerked the Maxima into reverse. He drove back about thirty feet, turning the wheel so he was facing the other cop, the state trooper he had first seen, who was now crouched and out in the open, with his drawn gun pointing right at Dixon. There was a flash from the muzzle of his pistol and the windshield spider-webbed, a hole the size of his fist appearing. Dixon felt something solid whiz past his left ear. Back into drive. He ducked under the dashboard and shot forward, until he was just under the pump, with its torn hose spilling gas out onto the stained grey concrete and mixing with the rain. The gasoline showered down on the Maxima. Dixon tossed his cigarette out onto the hood of the car and watched as an instant fireball erupted on the hood.

Now what? Decision time again. The state trooper who had fired at him was trying to get a better shot, maneuvring round to the side, looking for cover. How had he gotten here? There must be a state trooper vehicle somewhere. Dixon noticed it through the flames, behind a dumpster at the carpet outlet next door. He slammed the car into drive and, with his head down and fire and debris showering the front seat, he drove the Maxima over a curb and into the carpet outlet's parking lot.

Now he was between the state trooper and the vehicle. There was no way the cop had taken the keys out. Dixon slithered over into his passenger seat and in one smooth movement booted the door open, grabbed his laundry bag and gun, and fell onto the tarmac. He rolled away from the Maxima, which was now becoming a ball of flame. He darted behind the state trooper's car, opened the door, threw his bag and gun on the passenger seat and started it up. He saw the state trooper staring at him as he backed it around the side of the carpet outlet, then slammed it into drive and careened out onto the highway.

There was an explosion and Dixon saw a plume of smoke in the rear-view mirror as he gunned the cop car up to ninety. That would be the end of the Maxima. The other car wasn't even pursuing – maybe the cops were trying to prevent the entire gas station from going up. Dixon was flying down a long, clear access road, nothing on either side of him, a sign for a highway up ahead. He could hear the radio crackling, some calm voices giving addresses. Up ahead, a red light, one lone van sitting at the light, its left turn signal on. Dixon looked down and saw a field of toggle switches, one of them marked "whoop", another "red and blue lights". He hit them both and pulled up behind the van.

WHOOOOOOOP, went the siren. He slammed on the brakes behind the van, took the keys out the ignition, grabbed his laundry bag and his gun, and went up to the driver's side door. The van driver was an unshaven man of about forty, staring at him with wide eyes.

"What's going on, sir?" he asked, trying to sound jovial.

"Get the fuck out of the van."

"I didn't do anything," the man said. "I wasn't speeding." Then he looked at Dixon, noticed his singed suit with smoke coming off it, saw the gun and the laundry bag, and knew there was something more than a little wrong with this scene.

Dixon pointed the gun at his head. "If you're still in this van in three seconds you're a dead man. Three . . . two . . ."

"Aaaaaargh . . . OK, OK," the man was screaming, fumbling for the door latch. He opened the van and nearly fell out onto the pavement. Dixon hopped in, put the van in drive and blew through the red light before the door was even closed.

OK . . . think . . . think. Dixon took a couple of deep breaths. The guy was going to go into the state trooper vehicle, and use the radio. Or maybe he had a cellphone in his pocket. Should have put a bullet through the radio. Too late now. The guy would tell them what kind of van to look for. There was an access ramp to a highway coming up, and off the exit ramp, Dixon could see two state trooper cruisers coming in the other direction. He soared up the access ramp just as the cruisers sped down the exit ramp going towards the gas station. He had three, maybe four minutes in this van tops. The second he got onto the highway, he noticed another exit ramp. Exit 383, Wilford. He took it, and found himself on another long road, this one full of businesses. Plumbing supplies, a DMV office, a fast-food place. The first traffic light he went through was green, and there was a small Dodge in his way, so Dixon swerved around it, going about seventy now. Up ahead, a small bank. With a cash machine. A woman in her mid fifties had stepped out of her car to use the machine.

Dixon squealed into the parking lot and slammed on his brakes right next to the lady. She had turned around to look at him as he threw his money bag through her open window. The car was running. Beautiful.

"You take that," he said, pointing to the van.

"No no no," the stunned woman was yelling as she watched him climb into her brand new maroon Cadillac and screech off. He glimpsed her in the rear view mirror, standing beside the cash machine with the money in her hand, staring like a statue as he screeched back out onto the highway.

42

OK, now what? The woman would go into the bank and call the cops. Five minutes max and they'd have an APB out on a maroon Cadillac. He drove about three blocks, then slowed down. An old diner, with seven or eight trailer trucks parked in a huge parking lot. He drove around the back and parked behind the trucks.

He exhaled. For the first time since the gas station he could hear himself breathe. His breathing was fast but not panicked.

The parking lot was quiet, the brief rain shower had let up, and Dixon sat in the Cadillac and listened to the occasional car hiss by, tires on wet pavement.

He wiped his face. He was covered in sweat, rain and gasoline. Look around, what do you see? The backs of several trailer trucks. He got out of the car, stealthily walked between two of the trucks, and stepped up and tried the passenger door on one of them. It was open. He hustled back to the car, got his laundry bag of money and his gun, and climbed into the truck's sleeper.

The sleeper was dirty and old, and the blankets and mattress smelled like sweat, but the truck was gloriously dark and quiet. He pulled the curtains shut, and, holding the gun across his chest, resting his head on the laundry bag, he began to relax.

Within minutes, he heard the door open, and the driver got in. Dixon was waiting with his gun pointed straight at the curtains, expecting the driver to look into the sleeper for something, but he heard the man making himself comfortable in his seat and then the engine fired to life. The whole truck vibrated as it was idling, while the driver sat in his seat doing paperwork. Dixon breathed quietly, aware that any slight gurgle or sneeze or bump of his head against the metal sides of the sleeper might invite a curious peek into the sleeper. Then he heard the driver cough, mumble something to himself, and put the truck in gear. They were moving off.

Elias White was running his fingers through Melissa Covington's hair as they lay naked on the floor of his living room, watching her watch the muted TV. He felt completely at peace, as if he and Melissa were lovers on their honeymoon.

So that was it, he thought, sex. That was what was missing from his life. In all those red-wine-soaked evenings sitting at his computer, feeling abandoned and miserable and as if he didn't measure up to the ideal of a college professor, that was really the only thing he was missing. He had thought it was Ann, who was off studying in Heidelberg and communicated with him far less than he wanted, and whose communications, when they came, lacked any warmth. Sometimes he imagined he could read in her letters some relief at last to be rid of him. Perhaps it was just his insecurity that made him read and re-read each of her e-mails looking for telltale signs of actual fondness. Perhaps Ann was thinking of him at this very minute, sitting alone in her chilly German apartment with a view of a grey brick wall. For the first time in months, the notion of Ann being out and about and enjoying herself didn't fill him with a stab of anxiety, because he could feel Melissa's warm body curled up next to him.

He felt Melissa's hand slide between his ass and the carpet and he arched his back with a laugh. "What are you doing?"

"I need the remote," she harrumphed. "Where'd it go?"

Elias looked quickly around the room, saw the remote by one of the overturned couch cushions on the other side of the room, where it had ended up during their initial passionate first kisses. In the excitement of her acceptance of his advance clawing at her clothing while she moaned softly, he had thrown the little device off the couch. As he nuzzled her neck, he'd been wondering if this was a nightly occurrence for her, slipping over to someone else's house and banging a virtual stranger. He'd wondered, as he unsnapped her bra, how many other lovers this high school girl had taken on in after-school trysts like these. Was this his official welcome to the neighborhood? Had Mr Cuthbertson, the fifty-ish accountant who was always tending to the rosebushes at the end of his driveway, been the recipient of a Melissa

Covington after-school visit at some point in the last few years? The intensity of the sex had convinced him, for a moment, that there was some special connection between the two of them, but now, as she flipped through the news channels looking for something more entertaining, he found himself wondering again.

"What channel are you looking for?"

"MTV," she said. "You only live next door, but it's like your cable system is totally different, or something."

"I have satellite."

"How do I get MTV?"

"I have no idea. I never watch it."

She flipped past a few more channels, each one showing something Elias would have happily watched, growing more and more frustrated. Finally she tossed the remote down and said, "I'm going home."

Elias was suddenly filled with the desire to stop her, to not be alone. Almost brutally, as if panicked, he grabbed the back of her hair and pulled her towards him, kissing her hard on the mouth, and was surprised when she responded with a pleasant moan, began to stroke his chest. Then she straddled him and smiled devilishly. "My parents will be coming home soon," she said.

"Fuck 'em," he said, suddenly realizing that this was the role expected of him, the rough and tough guy who lived next door and didn't care. Didn't care that he was banging his next-door neighbor's underage daughter while trying to get himself on the national scene as a college professor published in respected journals.

Melissa Covington giggled and pressed her mouth against his. "I like you," she said.

Dixon lay still, the gun across his chest, feeling the truck hit every bump, sliding from one end of the sleeper to the other every time the truck took a turn, actually bumping his head when the turns were sharp. He never uttered a peep. Once, when the driver had to apply the brakes forcefully, Dixon felt himself nearly being pitched through the curtain; he came to a merciful stop just an instant before he was flung onto the gearshift. He lay still after that, able to see the driver through the crack in the sleeper curtain, watched him curse the "darned four-wheeler" in front of him that had necessitated the sudden stop. For a few moments, he didn't slither quietly back to the rear of the sleeper, enjoying this moment of voyeurism, the rare chance to see another person completely unaware of being observed. When the driver picked up the CB and called another trucker, Dixon shifted cautiously back to the rear of the sleeper to listen to the conversation.

"Hey, Jojo, what in God's name have you been doing in this cab?" the trucker called out. "It stinks of gasoline."

"Gasoline?" came the reply.

"Yeah. What's up with that?"

47

"I got no idea, pardner. Didn't smell o' nothin' last time I was in it."

There was a confused silence after that, and for a second Dixon was fearful that the curtain would come peeling back and he would be forced to confront the driver searching for the source of the smell. But the truck was still barreling down a road of some kind, apparently a mountain slalom course from the way Dixon was being flung around, and when the conversation started up again, it was, of all things, about the Bible.

"This is what you may eat of everything that is in the waters: Everything that has fins and scales," the trucker yelled into the CB.

"Everything in the waters that has no fins and scales is a loathsome thing to you," responded the other trucker. It was some kind of game they played, one of them quoting a passage from the Bible and the other responding with the next relevant passage. They were Texans all right. Or Oklahomans. Dixon thought about the Bible-thumpers he had known in prison, sycophantic ass-lickers so desperate to grovel before the Parole Board that they would actually learn these passages in an attempt to prove themselves cured. They were complicit in indulging the Parole Board's fantasy that getting raped in the shower, getting yelled at and beaten by the high-school dropouts employed as correctional officers actually cured you of anything.

Dixon stifled an urge to leap from behind the curtain with his pistol drawn and scream, "BOO! I'm God!" The only thing stopping him was the certainty that the shock would cause the trucker to go careening off whatever apparent winding mountain pass they were on.

"The Lord will provide," said the trucker, responding to something he heard over the CB. Something unintelligible came back.

"Amen to that," said the trucker.

"Amen," Dixon heard.

"Hey, Jojo, I'm going to pull over at the Flying J. I know it's only thirty more miles to Concord, but I need a bite. And I need to find out where this gas smell is coming from."

"Amen, my brother," came the reply, the guy still high on religion.

"I'll see you in Concord."

Concord! New fucking Hampshire! Dixon knew his state capitals from a guy he had celled up with some years back, a guy named Erwin who had hung a map in their cell. They were going in the right direction. All this while, he had been going towards Canada. Luck, at last, had finally caught up with him. This guy was going to pull over in a truck stop in New Hampshire!

And the minute he pulled over, he was probably going to pull the curtains back. Dixon was going to have to think of something then.

A few moments later, he felt the truck slowing down, then come to a complete stop. Dixon exhaled softly, surprised at how relaxing it felt not to be moving for a few seconds. Then the trucker put the vehicle in reverse, and he was tossed forward again, almost to the curtain. Then it was parked. He felt the vibration of the idling engine as he heard the trucker shuffle around in his seat. What the hell was the guy doing? Any second, Dixon waited for the curtain to be yanked back and the guy would find him there, a gasoline-soaked stranger in his sleeper.

But the door opened, and Dixon heard the trucker exit the cab with the engine still idling.

This was it. His big chance to escape. Dixon sat up and was suddenly paralyzed by a stabbing pain that shot down his right arm, which he had hardly moved in the six hours since he had jumped into the truck. He gasped and banged his head against the back of the sleeper, holding his arm. When he moved again he was prepared for the pain, but it was no less intense. Jesus, what the fuck had happened to him? He put his hand inside his jacket and felt warm liquid. He was bleeding.

Oh, Christ. He had been hurt. The car. Maybe broken glass from the Maxima. Maybe anything. He grabbed the laundry bag and grunted as he threw himself into the passenger seat, another wave of pain almost making him vomit. What the hell was this? It hadn't hurt the whole ride up here. Almost six hours. And NOW it hurt? He opened the passenger door and looked out, between two trailer trucks, where the trucker had parked. No one around, and no driver in the truck next to him, either. He hopped down quickly and shut the door, holding his laundry bag and gun. Another stab of pain, and he dropped the gun. He winced, and picked it up, then quickly stuffed the gun in his pants and pulled his jacket over it.

Dixon heard the footsteps of the driver as he checked everything, walking thoughtfully all around the truck. He could hear the guy coming around the end of the trailer, and he quickly ducked under another truck next to them and came out the other side, next to a field. He saw the trucker's legs as the guy walked slowly along his own truck, examining it as it idled. Then the trucker walked up to his passenger door and stopped.

He must have found something, Dixon decided. He felt like bolting, getting the hell out of there, but he stood for an extra second, looking underneath the truck at the trucker's legs as he stood by his passenger door. Then the trucker leaned over, clearly staring at something. The man kneeled down and looked at a spot on the ground very intently. What the fuck was it? Blood? Dixon backed up quietly, going under the next truck along, into total darkness, but he could still see the trucker as he picked something up off the ground.

Dixon saw the shape and recognized immediately what it was. A neatly wrapped stack of hundred dollar bills. Shit. It must have spilled out of the laundry bag. He backed up further and went under the next truck. The fucking Bible-thumper was going to call the cops, who would trace the money to the New Jersey bank robbery and then start looking here, in the boonies in New Hampshire. But just as he crawled under the trailer of the last truck in the row . . .

"Hallelujah," he heard the trucker scream, and Dixon knew the cops were not going to be called. "Hallelujah! The Lord has provided."

Ignoring the pain in his arm, Dixon took off running across the field.

3

Peace. Quiet. Night.

Just a few hundred yards from the bright lights of the truck stop, Dixon walked through the soggy bog of an empty field, not knowing or caring in which direction he was heading. He needed things. Food. A shower, a change of clothes, a place to rest. A way to look at, and fix, whatever the hell had happened to his arm. This was farm country, much like where he had grown up, but the grass was thicker and felt damp, not dry and dusty. Far off, he heard a cow mooing. There had to be a barn around. He went under a fence and through a copse of trees, and didn't see a farmhouse or a barn anywhere, just more open space. He wandered on. The noise of the truck stop faded, then disappeared altogether, and then all he could hear were his own footsteps and the occasional chirping of crickets.

Another fence. This time he anticipated the pain in his arm and he held it against him, tendered it, as he slid under the lowest rung of barbs. He could smell the cow shit now, but still no barn, no farmhouse. How big were these farms? The pain in his arm was intense, but he knew what movements exacerbated it now and it was becoming familiar. Each step he took sent a dull throb from the inside of his bicep up into his shoulder, the pain radiating in a dull wash of misery along the top of his back and his shoulder blades. He gritted his teeth. Wasn't so bad.

Through some trees, off in the distance, he could make out a car approaching along a road. The car was moving fast, maybe fifty or so, meaning the road was paved. Meaning it led somewhere worth going. Houses, barns, garages. Places to hide. Dixon walked through the dull, cloudy moonlight until he came to trees alongside the road, peered cautiously through them. The last thing he wanted now was an encounter with some people. He was too tired and pain-racked to pull his pistol out and horrify anyone into submission now. Robbing people at gunpoint took an intensity he knew he could no longer muster.

These first hours of the escape were the danger hours, when most robbers on the run got caught. No bank robber could sustain the mental intensity of evading the police for very long in that first desperate stage. Ten hours at the most, and even that was pushing it. It was like being a quarterback in the Super Bowl, or pitching a no-hitter. Your head had to be in the game every second or you were going to get dusted. Dixon had already been on the run a good eight hours now. Even the energy and discipline required to stay still in the back of the sleeper, to not reveal his presence, had drained him. That was why the cops rarely got into high-speed chases anymore. They knew that the soul-sucking concentration of continually wondering if you were being watched, of having to behave so that no one noticed you, of keeping your eyes out for every vehicle that had lights on top, had caught more criminals than any turbo-charged police cruiser.

But Dixon had experience on his side, because this was the third time he had been in this situation. He knew not to use phones. He knew that any idea that occurred to someone on the run was just a mirage. There was no help coming, there was just you, your sharp mind, and your ability to take pain.

In Wingate, Oklahoma, when he was twenty-four, after knocking off an armored car, he had called his girlfriend to tell her he'd be home soon. As he had approached her run-down trailer later that night, Dixon had noticed a police cruiser a few trailers down, backed up into an alley. Someone had parked it with the intention of concealing it. If it had just been out in the street, Dixon would have thought it was a cop car paying a visit to another trailer, and not paid it any mind. But this looked like a trick. He had taken off running, and the car peeled out after him. He had gotten away easily, but if he had just walked thirty seconds closer without noticing the car, things would have turned out differently.

What had happened that day, Dixon wondered, as he set off along the paved but unlit New Hampshire road? Had she put up a fight when the cops came, lied to them, tried to get them to leave? Had she secretly hoped that Dixon had gotten away? Or had she been friendly and helpful? Danielle Wiley, that had been her name. Pretty, petite, but already a little world-weary at the age of nineteen. She had wanted to be a hairdresser. She had been working as a waitress in the roadside diner where Dixon had gotten his first post-prison employment, trying to save up the money for beauty school. For her, there had never been any question that Dixon wasn't a pillar of the community, because she had been there the day Dixon's parole officer came by to question the manager about his attendance. Dixon had never been late or absent from work, and had been really trying to get his life back together, working the flat grill on the late shift. The parole officer had left satisfied that Dixon would soon be fully rehabilitated.

"You're coming along," he had said to Dixon that night, as they both stood out by the dumpster, smoking.

Dixon had said nothing. I'm coming along? He was yet another success story of the legal-correctional system, which had tried and convicted him, and then let him remain in jail even after his innocence was known. By this point Dixon knew it was all about success stories, not about success. The appearance of rehabilitation was

56

more important than the rehabilitation itself. To hate their guts was irrelevant. They expected it. But Dixon understood that showing them you hated their guts was more of a crime than crime. So he did what five years in prison had taught him to do, the dance of the shit-eaters: he shifted his feet and looked at the ground and grunted.

"You need anything?" the PO had asked.

It was such a friendly question, but Dixon understood it. Do I need anything? As in, show me your weakness, so I can control you better. Who would ask their PO for anything? What could a PO possibly provide that any con would need? Five years of my fucking life back would be nice, you pencil-pushing wannabe-tough-guy bag-of-shit with your middle-aged gut and your taxpayer-bleeding pension plan for twenty years of pretending to give a fuck . . .

"Nah," said Dixon.

"I think that girl in there's got her eye on you," the man said, but Dixon had had enough of their warm bonding session, enough of pretending they were two guys on the same side of the fence, looking out at the world. The PO hadn't just done five years in lockup, for nothing. The PO had a car. The PO drove around town trying to catch guys using drugs and skipping work, and trying to trick them into telling him things about themselves that would go into their files. There was no fence in the world of which they were on the same side. Dixon flicked his cigarette into the dumpster and opened the torn, battered screen door into the diner kitchen.

"I gotta get back to work," he said. "Dinner rush."

But he had been surprised to hear that the PO had thought Danielle had noticed him, because he had been wondering about it himself. He had noticed her the first day he had been hired there, was sure he would never have a chance with her, and had decided to put it out of his mind. He had to focus on work, earning some cash, keeping his record clean, putting all that shit behind him. And there really used to be days when he thought he could put the whole prison episode behind him, and just go to college, and maybe get a degree in engineering so he could build bridges. Since prison, he had become intrigued with bridges. Through the chain-link rec-yard fence he had been able to see a complex suspension bridge being built over a dam in the distance. That's what he would do, he thought, on one of those rare days when he imagined a future: manage a bridge-building team. He didn't need to get rejected by some nineteen-year-old diner waitress whose great dream was to work in a barbershop and who thought he was a seedy con like the guys he had known in lock-up. Just get by. Mind your own business, keep your ears open but your head down, just like in prison.

"Who was that guy?" Danielle asked him after the rush, when it was quiet but for the two of them cleaning up. He was scrubbing pans by the sink and she was wiping down the stainless steel waitress area right next to him.

"What guy?" Dixon asked without looking up.

"That guy you were talking to."

They had never talked before, and her question seemed to Dixon to be a demand for information, not casual conversation. It was the way the police demanded information, and he felt rage boiling in him. He turned to face her, and the rage dissipated in a flash. He had never really looked at her before, made eye contact from up close. From time to time he had risked furtive glances as she refilled customers' water glasses, or watched her body as she walked by with a heavy tray, but he had never had an opportunity to really see her face. It was pretty and honest and open and tired, and in that second he felt his anger evaporate, and that she just wanted a friend.

"He's my parole officer," Dixon said, as a rush of emotion hit him and the fury of moments ago turned to something else, like grief. He suddenly found himself stemming back a flood of tears. He turned away from her and busied himself with the wet, cleaned pans, as if he had to dry them and put them away immediately. It only took a second to compose himself, but he was horrified. Nothing like that had ever happened before.

"Are you OK?" she asked.

"I'm fine . . . got some cleaning shit in my eyes." He stared down into the soapy water.

"What are you doing later?"

"Later when?" He was still turned away from her, but he had composed himself now. Her question was odd, because after a mention of a parole officer, the conversation, in Dixon's experience, would always take the same course. What did you do? How long were you in for? Blah blah blah. But she wasn't interested.

"After work. Are you on work release or are you out?"

Obviously this girl knew a little something about the correctional system. "I'm out," he said.

"Why don't you come over and have a beer?"

He turned to face her again, a little panicked by the offer. What did she want from him? Was this some kind of a set-up? Would some guy with prison tats leap out from behind a curtain and stab him and rifle his pockets for his nine dollars and change?

"Awright."

She had nodded and walked off. Later he had gone back to a run-down trailer which Danielle had been proud of, because she was able to live there without support from anyone else. She had smiled when showing him the garden, which coyotes had just destroyed, and laughed when pointing out the hole in the trailer wall covered with a bed sheet; but she was proud of the place. Dixon remembered looking at the trashed trailer and wondering if he would ever have this much independence, this much freedom. Then she smoked a joint on the stoop while he watched, wanting more than ever to share it but knowing the hot drug test would send him back for five more years. Then they went to bed together.

They had been dating two years, and were talking of marriage, when the armored car job came up. He could buy her a real diamond ring and the job would be smooth and quick, and he could quit the goddamned diner and they could live in Mexico or change their names. He never asked her about it, figured it might be best to show her the money first – forty grand, real cash. That would be an argument-winner right there, if he had the cash first. He doubted she would scream and yell much when the opportunity for a better life was right in front of her, in a laundry bag. So he went up to Oklahoma with three guys from the joint, swearing allegiance to each other as they drove along the highway to Wingate. After the robbery got fucked up and two of them got caught, Dixon knew that he didn't have much time, that the allegiance-swearing session was all for show, that the two guys were in an interrogation room at that very minute flipping through mug books for Dixon's picture. They had never told each other their real names. He had gotten away with $1,800, and he called Danielle to tell her that his visit to his aunt was over and he'd be coming home, and her voice had sounded just a bit off-centre, like she didn't really care that much. Like there were cops in the room right then, and maybe the PO – the PO, who always wanted to help, probably trying to look down Danielle's shirt as he leaned over her, his fingers on the handcuffs he kept on his belt. It was over then, Dixon knew, but he didn't admit it to himself, though he had been smart enough to keep his eye out for cop cars from the moment he entered her street.

You couldn't make phone calls. You took the pain, you took the hunger, you kept walking.

Five miles passed. There was a town coming up, Dixon knew, because the cars were driving by every few minutes now. He had to keep ducking into the woods. He went over a hill, and in the clouded moonlight he could read a sign that said Tiburn College, 4. Then he saw a row of houses, a quiet, tree-lined street off to his left. He crossed the street and walked through a field, and through the trees he could see lights on in most of the houses.

Common sense: the house with the fewest lights has the fewest people. The third house down had just a TV flickering in the living room. Dixon crept through the trees, careful not to step on any sticks or piles of dead leaves, his senses alert now, the pain in his side less

62

noticeable. He checked the houses to the right and the left. Two lights on in each, one upstairs, one downstairs. Just the TV flickering in the third house. He drew closer, until he was at the edge of the unfenced backyard.

No dogs barking, but you could never be too sure. A dog would ruin everything right now. If there were no dogs, he could get inside the middle house, but he'd have to wait until the person or people watching the TV went to bed. What to do if there's a dog? Take off running again, Dixon figured.

He sat down far enough back in the trees to remain hidden, even if someone came out onto the back deck. As he leaned his head back against the cold, hard bark, a wave of exhaustion hit him. He was running out of steam, he knew. He'd lost some blood. He couldn't wait out the night here, he'd pass out. The neighbors would find him torn and bloody under a tree with a pistol in one hand and a bag of money in the other. Think they'd find that suspicious? Get the fuck up, he told himself. No sleeping here.

Dixon struggled to his feet and walked as cautiously as he could over to the window with the flickering lights. Friday, the best day for a bank robbery, was also the worst for a home invasion, because everybody stayed home on a Saturday morning. Couldn't sit and wait for people to go to work. Maybe some guy in this house had fallen asleep in front of the TV, and he wasn't getting off the couch until tomorrow morning. The window was wide and low, and if Dixon approached the house at the right angle he would be able to see in.

The night was so quiet that he could hear the TV clearly. The window was open. Damn, now he'd have to be extra quiet. There was some canned laughter. More dialog, more canned laughter. Dixon could see the couch now. There was nobody on it. This was weird. Had they just left the TV on for a pet? Just as he was about to go right up to the window and peer in, an arm came into view and dropped down again. The fucker was on the floor!

He heard a man sigh. Then a girl stood up, naked, and looked around. "Have you seen my bra?" Dixon clearly heard her ask.

Dixon was right out in the open. If they turned on a light, it would illuminate him right in the middle of the yard. Fortunately, a loud, braying commercial came on at that very second, and Dixon used the excessive noise to cover a quick approach to the side of the house. He hunkered down just outside the open window, where he could see in, but duck down if need be.

He felt his heart thumping and heard his breathing coming too heavily, and he made an effort to breathe quietly. The girl was still looking for her bra. "It was a sports bra," she was saying. "It was really expensive. I can't go home without my bra, my parents'll kill me."

Her parents? What was going on here? The man stood

up, and Dixon got a full view of him. Early to mid-thirties, physically fit but slight, not the kind to do manual labor. He had an air of daintiness about him.

"Look under the couch," he said.

The girl found her bra and they both began dressing. She pulled on a loose-fitting sports T-shirt, on which Dixon could clearly read the words "West Tiburn High School Lacrosse".

"I think I got everything," she said, picking up a book bag.

The man went over and stood next to her, reached down and kissed her. "Bye," he said.

"If my parents ask, you were just helping me with my homework."

"Why would they ask?"

"I'm just saying. If they ask."

"OK. What were we studying?"

"Physics."

"I'm not good at physics."

"Look, just tell them that," said the girl, sounding exasperated. "They don't know what you're good at. They just know you're a professor." Even without the T-shirt, Dixon could tell she was a high school girl by her exaggerated emotion.

This was getting interesting. And useful. Dixon didn't get to be a thirty-nine-year-old career criminal by not knowing how to make lemons out of lemonade.

"Bye," the girl said quickly. Then she looked around the room. "Do you smell that?"

"Smell what?"

"Coming from outside," she said as she left toward the front door. "It smells like gasoline. Did you leave the grill on, or something?"

"The grill's propane," said the man. "And I haven't grilled anything today." Their voices grew fainter as they left into the front hall.

"Seeya," he heard the girl say, and then the sound of the front door closing. The girl's footsteps grew fainter, then, as Dixon was about to go around the side of the house, they grew louder again. She was going to the house next door. A motion detector triggered a light on her front porch as Dixon watched her take some keys out of a bag and fumble with them for a second, then let herself in.

Well I'll be damned, Dixon thought. Mr Professor here is banging his neighbor's daughter. Mr Professor came back into the living room – Dixon ducked back down again – and this time he seemed to be sniffing the air. Then he walked over to the window, closed it, turned off the TV and went upstairs to bed.

Elias White was having a bad dream. The instant he awoke from it, he could hardly remember it, but he knew it was bad. He was trapped inside something, he

66

remembered that much. Maybe people were poking him with sticks and taunting him. He didn't want to remember, shook his head and blinked, and became aware of an overpowering odor of gasoline in the dark room.

"What in God's name *is* that?" he mumbled to himself. He turned over on his pillow, hoping it would go away. He took a few deep breaths, but the gasoline odor nearly made him gag. Irritated, he reached up and turned on the lamp on the bedside table.

And screamed.

And instinctively made some attempt to shrink up into a fetal position, his legs kicking savagely under the heavy covers.

"Hi," said Dixon.

Sitting in Elias White's father's favorite velvet-covered chair was a man who stank of gasoline, his face and hands caked with blood, wearing a torn and rumpled business suit and holding a big silver pistol. He was smiling.

"Who . . . who . . . ohmigod."

"Settle down a minute," said Dixon. "Just relax and don't say nothin'. We're just going to sit here and look at each other for a few minutes, OK?"

"OK." Elias could feel his heart racing, almost painfully. He opened his mouth and took in gulps of air, feeling himself about to black out.

"Breathe easy," said Dixon. Elias found his voice oddly comforting, confident and almost paternal. But obviously it was a delusion, because this man was a psychopath who broke into people's bedrooms in the middle of the night, and he was planning some psychopathic thing. So the voice didn't really matter. He had clearly been doing psychopathic shit to people for a long time. Elias could tell there was no reaction he could have that this man hadn't seen before, which was why the intruder seemed so confident. So the low-key, relaxed manner, which Elias knew was supposed to make him feel at ease, was actually giving him the chills.

He waited for the man to talk, but the man didn't talk, just looked. He had an intelligent eye, was taking in not only Elias but everything around the room. The bedroom was small, and the furniture had mostly been chosen by Elias's mother some thirty-five years before. The man was looking at the hope chest at the end of the bed, then at the Indian-motif bedspread, which had been a gift from Ann a few years ago. And then at the ceiling, where a carpenter had recently replaced the broad, maple beams.

"What's your name?" the man said finally.

Elias breathed out, long and hard. "Elias. Elias White."

"My name's Phil Dixon," the man said, and Elias noticed a heavy southern or western accent. Not from around here. He was holding the gun loosely, Elias saw, as if he wasn't terribly concerned with it right now. That had to be a good sign.

"I got some problems, Elias," the man said.

Elias nodded. He didn't want to hear what was next. He imagined the man was going to reveal he heard voices, voices instructing him to kill people in their bedrooms, and that if he didn't do it some terrible shit would happen to him.

"I want you to help me with them."

Elias nodded again. Oh god, here comes the psychopathic shit. Elias noticed a black laundry bag at the man's feet bulging with something. Probably rope and knives and duct tape. If this guy came a foot closer, Elias was going to start screaming and fighting and . . .

"Are you a doctor, by any chance?"

"A doctor?" Elias's voice was almost a whisper. "I have a doctorate . . . In history."

"That's about as fucking useless as it gets," Dixon said, almost conversationally. "You want to hear about my problems?"

Elias nodded. What the hell else was he going to do? Here it comes. He's going to tell me about his weirdness and then try to do some shit to me with whatever is in that black bag.

"A cop in New Jersey shot me today."

That wasn't too weird. Sounded pretty rational, in fact. And it explained the blood dripping off the chair onto the white throw rug.

"I think I'm losing a lot of blood," he said.

"Yeah," White said, suddenly thinking the situation might not be as unmanageable as he first suspected. He pointed at the throw rug. "I think you are."

"I'm gonna need some blood, Elias. A one-pint bag of type A positive blood. Do you follow?"

"I'm O negative," Elias said.

"I don't want *your* blood, you fuckhead," Dixon snapped, and it made Elias feel surprisingly more at ease. The easygoing persona that Elias had feared developing into pure evil weirdness had been replaced by a human with emotions, someone whom Elias could reason with and understand. As soon as he heard the word fuckhead, Elias White knew he was going to live through the night. "What do you think, I want you to be my donor?"

Elias just stared.

Dixon continued slowly, as if he were talking to an idiot. "I want a pint of type A positive blood. Maybe two. I want a professional, a phlebotomist or a nurse, to give it to me using sterilized surgical equipment. I want someone who knows what the fuck they're looking at to have a look at this bullet wound. I think the bullet went through me, but I need some shit put in there to

70

prevent infection. I need it all bandaged up and I need it done right. And most of all . . . most of fucking all . . . are you listening?"

Elias nodded.

"I want some fucking painkillers."

Elias nodded again. "They have all those things at the hospital," he suggested. "Would you like me to drive you there?"

Despite himself, Dixon laughed. The laughter caused a pain to shoot through his side, and he winced.

"No, I don't want you to drive me to the hospital. But I do want something to eat. Let's go downstairs and get something to eat. We'll talk while we eat. I'm fucking starvin'."

"Eggs," said Dixon as he pulled up a chair at the kitchen table. "Cheese and eggs and sausages, if you got 'em." He was no longer pointing the gun at Elias, because by now the guy knew he had it, and that was usually enough. You didn't need to keep making your point. But Dixon did need to watch the exit routes, back up the stairs or through the back door, and he chose the chair with the best view of both. Elias looked like he wasn't much of a fighter, but Dixon figured he could move pretty fast if escape became an option.

"I've got eggs, but no cheese or sausages," said Elias.

"Make what you've got."

71

Dixon watched Elias's hands as he took the eggs out of the fridge. They were shaking slightly. A little fear was good. If they were shaking too much, Dixon would have to sit him down, talk to him again, calm him down. He wanted a rational conversation, not the usual sobbing and begging. If they weren't shaking at all, that would be bad, too. You had to be extra careful if the hostage wasn't scared.

Elias fired up the frying pan, threw in some butter. He was preoccupied enough with cooking now that Dixon could start talking again.

"Who's that little filly you're carrying on with next door?"

Elias had been about to crack an egg over the frying pan. He stopped and stared. "She's a friend," he said finally.

"A friend, huh?" Dixon leaned back in his chair. "You get naked on the floor with all your friends?"

Elias broke two eggs and looked at him, as if wounded by the remark. "Is this what you do, then? Go around and spy on people?"

Dixon laughed, enjoying himself. He could tell when people were acting. This guy was angry, but didn't have the steel to show anger, so he went with playing hurt. Dixon leaned back in his chair and drank in the warm, greasy smell of the eggs, aware that his mouth was watering. God, he was hungry. "How old is that girl, anyway?"

72

"Early twenties," muttered Elias. "Or something like that. She locked herself out."

Dixon had held enough people hostage at gunpoint for long enough to know a danger period was approaching. Elias had already undergone a minor attitude shift. He had become accustomed to being a hostage, now, and his mind was starting to whir. Dixon could read his eyes and body language. His speech had dropped in volume, a sign that he was trying to speak and think at the same time. He was thinking of poisonous things he could put in the eggs. It was natural. Dixon didn't hold it against him, but he did say, "When you hand me those eggs, if there's anything on the plate but eggs, I'm gonna shoot you before I eat 'em."

Elias looked at him, wide-eyed with the terror that Dixon had noticed subsiding.

"That includes salt and pepper."

"I'm just frying eggs," Elias said, with such an exaggerated sense of innocence that Dixon knew he had pegged him dead on.

"Well, keep fryin' 'em, then."

"OK."

This guy had been showing a little fire, but now it was out again. He was going to be a great hostage. He had very little steel in him, Dixon figured, the type of guy who lasted in prison by hooking himself up with the

White Aryan Brotherhood so the coons wouldn't use him for a sex toy. He wasn't even as clever as he seemed at first glance. Professor or not, Dixon liked his chances at staying one step ahead of him.

"Early twenties, eh?" Dixon asked. "I put her at about sixteen, tops."

"She's older than that," Elias said, staring at the eggs.

"Let's you and me stop the bullshit," Dixon said, as Elias dumped the eggs unceremoniously on a plate and tossed the plate down in front of Dixon with enough force for him to be able to detect a burning hostility. Showing fire again. Good. And he was going to put it out again. "Get me some fucking shit to eat with," he said with a motion of the pistol. Elias dug into the drawer for some silverware and Dixon wolfed down the two eggs in about five seconds. "Make some more."

Elias opened the fridge and cracked six more eggs as Dixon continued talking.

"As I said, let's stop the bullshit, OK? That girl is the neighbor's daughter and she's not sixteen yet and you and I know it . . ."

"She's seventeen," snapped Elias.

"Oh, now she's seventeen. A minute ago she was in her early twenties."

Elias stared at him, and Dixon knew he was reeling from being tricked so easily.

"I even doubt that. I think sixteen tops."

"What do you care?" Elias asked, with a hint of resignation, like he already knew the answer.

"What's the age of legal consent around here?" asked Dixon.

Elias said nothing.

"What if it's eighteen?" Dixon pushed. "That'd put you and me on the same side of the law, wouldn't it?"

Elias dropped several eggs onto Dixon's plate, then a couple onto his own, and sat down across the table. "What did you do, anyway? I mean, why did a cop shoot you?"

Dixon felt he had made his point and permitted the subject change. Blackmail was a sleazy affair, and he wouldn't even touch it were he not so desperate. He wanted the discussion over with. "I have a career in weapons-based financial reallocation."

"I . . . I've never heard of that."

"I rob banks."

Elias nodded, as Dixon watched him piece it together. "So you robbed a bank today?"

"I did."

"And afterwards you decided to come to my house?"

"Wasn't a decision, really. Just wound up here."

"Hmm," said Elias, finishing his eggs, standing up and putting the plate in the sink. "So that black laundry bag . . . that's . . ."

"The money," said Dixon. He realized that this information was comforting Elias, that this small-town college professor had expected to be killed, but was now noticing a logical thread behind Dixon's actions. He was starting to understand The Deal. "You let me stay here for two weeks, until this wound heals up, until I get my shit together and everyone stops looking for me, and I don't say a word about the girl. Sound like a deal?"

Elias was looking at him, and Dixon could read his thoughts. To agree would be to admit that he wanted the incident with the girl kept quiet. Up until now, he had been pretending it was no big deal, that he wouldn't care if the whole town knew. But Dixon was from a small town, too, and he knew better. Especially this guy; young, ambitious, aggressive. Dixon didn't know how long this little affair had been going on, but he knew people weren't supposed to know.

"If my parents ask, you were just helping me with my homework," Dixon said, mimicking Melissa's voice.

Elias shook his head, pale. "Jesus, how long were you out there?"

"Long enough. Look, this is an old house. I'll throw in a couple of thousand to help you fix it up after I've left." Dammit, why did he just offer that? Guilt over the blackmail, over making this man put his head in his hands. Why had that been necessary? Who hadn't sinned? "You keep your mouth shut about me being here, I'll keep my mouth shut. Got it?"

Elias took Dixon's plate. "Two weeks?" he said, as if he had a choice.

"I'll be gone in two weeks."

Elias shrugged as he began washing the plates, his shoulders hunched. "You gotta take a shower, though. You must take a shower. Now. You're making my whole house stink of gasoline."

It took him half an hour to get his clothes off. The dress shirt had sealed itself into his wound as the blood had dried, and he had to carefully peel the cotton away from the bloody, damaged skin, and as he gently yanked out each thread it was a new experience in agony. Tears streamed down his face and blood started pouring down his ribcage and splattering on the white linoleum tiles of the bathroom floor. By the time he was finally naked, the pain had exhausted him to the point that all he could do was slump against the cool porcelain of the bathtub, his tear-streaked face pressed against the tiles.

The bathroom looked like a slaughterhouse. He had splattered blood on the mirror, in the sink, on the toilet, all over the floor. His gasoline-drenched clothes lay in a pile.

It felt good to be naked and alone. You were who you were when you were naked and alone. No need to pretend. You didn't have to be a businessman, you didn't have to be tougher than the next guy, you didn't have to make anyone fear or respect you. He would rather be naked and bleeding in this bathtub than anywhere he had been in the last ten years. He was free.

With a sigh, Dixon pulled himself up and looked in the mirror. He still wasn't used to seeing himself without the beard and long hair. He looked younger, he thought. He looked young and scared and tired and pale and he was losing blood like a gut-shot steer.

He heard Elias drop something outside the door. "I put some clothes there for you," Elias said. "And some towels."

Dixon was too tired to answer. He turned the water on, adjusted the temperature, and stepped into the shower, gingerly keeping his wound away from the hot spray. Even the slightest trickle of water going into the wound was a shock of pain like he hadn't felt before. Or at least for a long while. With the warm water beating down on his neck and shoulders, he looked at the wound for the first time and he could see the story behind it.

A small hole started at his back, about five inches down from his shoulder blade. The bullet had never really gone in, but torn flesh all around as it had grazed his side right up near his bicep. Then there was more flesh tearing on the inside of the bicep, just a nasty mess, as if someone had decided to pound a hamburger with a claw hammer rather than throw it on a grill. Dixon figured that if he had been an inch to the right, and he had been holding his arm farther from his side, the bullet would have just passed between his arm and ribcage. Of course, that type of thinking was pointless. If he'd been an inch to the left it would have gone through his lung, or two inches to the right and it would have hit his arm dead on, puncturing his brachial artery or breaking the humerus.

He got out of the shower, got the clothes and towels from outside the door, gingerly dried himself and began to dress. Elias had left him a pair of oversized blue sweat pants and an extra large white T-shirt with the words "Tiburn County Fair" emblazoned across the chest, with a colorful picture of a Ferris wheel. Probably the only things he had which would fit Dixon. They were about the same size, but Dixon had a lot more muscle, and doubted whether he could fit into any of Elias's regular clothes.

This was a crucial time, Dixon knew. He had left Elias alone for over an hour. When he opened the shower door, if there were no policemen in the living room, waiting for him, then The Deal had been made. He was confident that Elias would go for it, but you never knew for sure. Maybe the offer of a few thousand dollars had clinched it. People liked money. He draped an oversized beach towel over his shoulders, making sure the end of the towel covered his left hand, concealing his pistol, which had the safety off. If there were cops out there, he wasn't going anywhere willingly.

Dixon pulled the bathroom door open, peered out and listened. Silence. He walked down the stairs, one step at a time, a second between each step, taking in the sounds. Nothing. Then a rattling of a newspaper. Didn't mean anything. When he hit the bottom stair, he turned and looked around into the living room. It was empty. Through the living room window, he could see that the sun was coming up.

Elias White was sitting at the kitchen table, reading the newspaper. He nodded when he saw Dixon. "I put some coffee on," Elias said. "You want some?"

Dixon sat down gingerly in the seat across from him. The air in the kitchen was still heavy from the greasy smell of fried eggs, which, mixed with the coffee, reminded him of the diner where he had worked, years ago.

"Yeah," he said. "Coffee would be good."

4

"I'll tell you how you're gonna get me all that shit I need. The A positive blood and painkillers and so on."

Elias shook his head. "I can't do that. I don't know anyone who does things like that."

"I'll show you how."

"You'll show me how? What're you talking about? I can't just walk into a convenience store and get those things. You need to take care of that yourself."

It was funny, Dixon thought, that this man, who was so persuadable when it came to sharing his house with a fugitive bank robber, was so resistant to performing simple tasks to help him. He understood the difference, though. Taking Dixon on as a temporary room-mate was a passive endeavor. Acquiring the help of a nurse, and getting controlled substances, was active. Once Elias agreed to something like this, he could no longer claim that he was a victim if the police ever got involved. More importantly, he couldn't claim it to himself, either.

Dixon reached into his laundry bag and took out a packet of freshly wrapped, hundred dollar bills. He broke the wrapping, counted off five bills and put them on the table. "You know any nurses?"

Elias looked like he was thinking hard. "Not really."

"Bullshit. You work at a college, right?"

"Yes. I'm a professor," Elias said distinctly, as if Dixon had failed to grasp the grandeur of the job.

"Well, don't they have an infirmary there?"

"Yes. But it's a small one."

"I don't give a fuck what size it is. There's a nurse there, right?"

"Yes, there's a nurse there."

"Well give her these and tell her to get me the shit I asked for. Then tell her to come over and clean out my wound. And she'll get the rest of this packet." Dixon waved the hundreds around and slapped them down on the table.

"She's not that kind of nurse," Elias said. Dixon was just staring at him, so he continued as if trying to explain something to a small child. "She's a nice, Jamaican woman. She's about forty-five or so. She hands out pills for headaches for the students and faculty. She doesn't do things like this."

Dixon nodded. "She's forty-five, huh?"

Elias nodded. "Around there."

"And Jamaican."

"Yes. She's Jamaican."

"So you know for a fact that forty-five-year-old Jamaican women don't break the law if you offer them five grand?"

82

Elias had thought that his rational argument was starting to win Dixon over. What the hell was this man thinking? He couldn't go wandering around the college campus getting people to commit crimes for him. He was a college professor on his way to Harvard.

"What age and nationality are we looking for?" Dixon asked. "Would a twenty-five-year-old American nurse be more likely to help me out? Or should we try older? Maybe a sixty-year-old Canadian. Do you know any sixty-year-old Canadian nurses? I hear they're a walking crime spree . . ."

"Look, you don't have to be sarcastic," Elias snapped. "I can't do this. These people up here . . . I don't know where you're from, but people here like to . . ." He trailed off.

"Like to what? Like to fuck underage girls?"

"Fuck you." Elias stopped, suddenly horrified by his own speech. He was expecting the gun to come out again, but Dixon just smiled.

"It'll be fun," said Dixon. "You just wave the money. The money'll do the talking for you." He pushed the hundreds towards Elias. "Five grand. You offer her three and a half to start, then raise it up if she protests. What's the big deal? I bet she's got access to all that stuff in the infirmary. Everybody thinks like you do . . . nice Jamaican woman. I bet nobody even watches her.

Christ, for all you know, she's probably dealing pills out of that infirmary."

"No she isn't," Elias said firmly.

Dixon looked at Elias and shook his head. "The world is full of vice, my friend. You think people look at you and think, hey, I bet that guy's doing his neighbor's underage daughter?"

"Look," Elias snapped. "She's not underage. She's seventeen. It just happened the one time, yesterday. That's it. It's not this sick, seedy affair like you keep making it out to be."

"I'm just making a point," Dixon said, smiling.

Elias sighed. He was going to have to ask his college infirmary nurse to clean out a fugitive's gunshot wound. Fear tightened his stomach at the thought of her refusal. He had a mental image of her running for the telephone to make the call that would ruin his carefully planned life. But there was something else mixed in with the fear. He had never done anything like this before.

"Exciting, isn't it?" said Dixon with a grin.

"No," Elias snapped, angry at having his thoughts read. "Risking my career is not exciting."

Dixon nodded. There was silence in the kitchen, then finally Dixon said, "It's Saturday." They both stared out the kitchen window and marveled for a moment at how the days of the week kept right on in sequence no matter the events in an individual life.

"I'm tired," Dixon said, and Elias sensed true exhaustion in his words, not just the physical aspects of sleep deprivation but a weariness with his life. This wasn't a man who enjoyed running from the law. "I need some sleep."

Elias looked up. "Where do you want to sleep?"

"How's the basement?" It was perfect for Dixon. He had peered down there while Elias was reading the paper. It had one entrance, unfinished stone walls, offering all the protection of a prison cell without any of the drawbacks. He liked the fact that you had to go down creaky stairs to get down there, which would give him plenty of noise and reaction time in case Elias decided to kill him in his sleep. Maybe he'd find some empty cans and put them on the stairs.

"I'm gonna go to sleep in the basement and you're going to take care of this nurse thing for me, OK?"

Elias shrugged. What else could he do? Besides, there was something about this gun-wielding maniac he was starting to trust. He seemed to have some kind of inner peace and confidence that his insane plans would actually work. Elias really did believe Dixon would leave in two weeks, and not kill him when the time came. If Dixon planned to kill him, why didn't he do it last night while he was sleeping? Then again, maybe Dixon was waiting for him to get the nurse. Maybe as soon as the nurse left, it would be two quick shots to the head and that would be the end of Elias White, up-and-coming young professor with a recently finished paper on the class struggle in Germany between the wars.

"I keep the money," said Elias.

"Say what?"

"I keep the money bag until you leave. I hide it somewhere safe, as protection. I have no guarantee you're not going to just kill me as soon as I get the nurse."

"So you're going to get the nurse? That was easy." Dixon smiled. "You can't have the money."

"Well then I won't get the nurse."

Dixon pulled the pistol out, and held it up. Elias froze. The look in Dixon's eye was different from anything he had seen before. His expression was softer and more calm. Here it comes, he thought. Oh, Jesus, what a way to die. Why had he been thinking about trusting this homicidal maniac? He tried to move his mouth to tell Dixon it was OK, he'd get the nurse, but his mouth didn't move. It was frozen shut, his jaw looking determined. His muscles had shut down, waiting for the bullet that was about to crash into his skull . . . Was this how his mother had died, quickly, one shot? Or had she been stabbed? Elias was suddenly gripped by grief, grief for his mother, grief for himself. Then he felt his muscles loosen up again, and he was about to start begging and screaming when Dixon smiled.

"Tell you what. You get me the nurse, and I'll give you the gun. But I keep the bullets . . . Jesus, son, you look as white as a ghost."

Dixon stared at him for a few more seconds, while Elias sat there feeling sheepish, and Elias could see Dixon piecing together the reason for Elias's expression. He watched Dixon's face as he gradually understood. A big grin spread across Dixon's face, then finally he laughed, a long, loud baritone laugh stopped short by a convulsion of pain from the movement.

Dixon winced hard and groaned. "Just get me the goddamned nurse, OK?"

"OK," Elias tried to say, but it just came out a whisper.

Driving into school on his day off, Elias began to wonder about his life. He had been convinced his life had been about to end and now he was alive, smelling things, hearing things, driving. What if Dixon had shot him? What would it all have added up to? His joy in experiencing his senses was diminished by a nagging doubt that he had not done nearly as much as he could have with his life.

He remembered his father's funeral, and his determination that day to change everything, to get himself on the map of academia. That had been nine years ago. What had he accomplished since then? He had started dating Ann, a bright young woman who would do well at the academic gatherings he attended, but his own career had stalled. Still no tenure and he was thirty-five. He was becoming the same boring, unconstructive layabout his father had been, trying to speak knowledgeably in lectures about things he only pretended to care about to a roomful of students who would gaze out the window at the trees changing colors.

His life was still going to waste. There was no part of German or American history that fired him up. There were, as educators claimed, no lessons to be learned. If humanity had learned such a great lesson from the Holocaust, why were the Cambodians involved in one of their own three decades later? Why were the Rwandans and Yugoslavs busy trying to butcher themselves to extinction in the 90s? His job was to put some kind of positive spin on studying history, as if reciting recorded facts about mass murder was in some way useful, as if it would ensure prevention of such madness in the future. Who was he kidding? Most of his students were nursing or computer-tech majors who had to take his course to fulfill an arts requirement – highly unlikely candidates to instigate genocide, and even if they were susceptible to behaving so savagely, Elias's course would just give them ideas.

He needed to get out of Tiburn. He needed to find a job with a future. He needed to get books and articles published and get tenure at a school people had heard of, instead of sitting around this one-horse New Hampshire shithole babbling nonsense to the local rich kids. He was almost glad that Dixon had come out of nowhere and waved a gun in his face. It was a jumpstart. It was going to get his life moving again. If the nurse called the police on him, he decided, it would be for the best. It would actually force him to leave town, to go and experience notoriety and respect in a place where it mattered.

He pulled up outside the infirmary. He could see the light on, knew there was someone inside. The nurse had to be on duty until five on Saturdays for the kids who lived in the dorms. He opened the door and saw her sitting at the desk in the entrance hall, filling out forms.

"Hi," Elias said, trying to put some confidence in his voice.

"Hello, Professor White," the nurse said with a heavy Jamaican accent. She was wearing blue scrubs and looked very professional, not the type of person who would be interested in the deal he was going to propose. "What brings you here on a Saturday?"

Elias patted the money in his pocket and realized he had nothing to say, hadn't rehearsed an approach. He couldn't just blurt out the request. He needed to lead up to it somehow. "Hi," he said again.

She was still sitting at her desk, looking up at him expectantly.

"What's your name?" he asked after what seemed to him to be an endless excruciating silence, but was in fact just a few seconds.

"I am Nurse Davenport," she said. She was still looking at him. "You are Professor White? We met last year. I gave you a flu shot."

Up until that moment Elias had completely forgotten about the flu shot. "Yes," he said. "Thank you. I didn't get the flu that winter."

"Those flu shots are very good," Nurse Davenport said in her lilting accent, which made every word sound wise and thoughtful.

"Yes," Elias agreed quickly. "Very effective."

Elias stood there for a few more seconds until finally Nurse Davenport, convinced he had just shown up to waste her time, turned her attention away from him and swiveled her chair over to a gray metal filing cabinet and began to pull a file from it. She swiveled the chair back and opened the file on her desk and began to look at it, pen in hand.

"Have you ever treated a gunshot wound?" Elias asked.

Nurse Davenport looked up patiently, and Elias was aware that had he been a student and not a professor, she would have told him she was busy and asked him to leave. But she nodded politely.

"Yes, I have," she said. "In Jamaica."

"People shoot each other a lot there, do they?" Elias was aware the question was idiotic, so he added, "I mean, I mean . . ."

"Sometimes," she said. "There are bad neighborhoods in Kingston. Shootings, stabbings. It can be crazy sometimes."

Silence again. But now Nurse Davenport was sensing there was something on Elias's mind, and she gave him a pleasant smile.

"Why you ask me this now, Professor White?"

"Elias, please."

She nodded. "Why you come in here on a Saturday ask me about gunshot wounds? You got one?"

"A friend of mine does," Elias said. He knew she had only been joking, but his earnest response didn't seem to surprise her.

"But you don't want to take him to the hospital, this friend?"

"Wouldn't be a good idea."

She nodded, understanding. This was going well. To make it go better, Elias added, "He wants to give you five thousand dollars if you can come over and, you know, take care of it."

"Where he shot?"

Oh, that was good. She didn't seem nearly as surprised as Elias was expecting her to be.

91

"Right here." Elias pointed to his rib and bicep. "It's been bleeding a lot and I think he needs some blood. He's A positive. And he wants painkillers . . . and . . ." Now the cat was out of the bag, Elias realized he couldn't stop talking. Nurse Davenport was staring at him. "He had a hunting accident," Elias added, surprising even himself.

"No," she shook her head. "He didn't have no hunting accident. You lying." She laughed.

Elias said nothing. OK, he wouldn't try anymore bullshit.

"The blood's no good. I can't get you A positive blood. You need a hospital for that. He'll just have to drink a lot of fluids. But I can come over and irrigate the wound, and clean it out for him. And put a bandage on. And give him painkillers."

"OK," Elias nodded, beaming. "When can you come?"

"After I get done here. An hour or two."

"Thank you," Elias said, relief pouring out of him. "Thank you so much. You're a lifesaver . . ."

"Five thousand dollars, right?"

5

Agent Denise Lupo leaned back in her chair in her cramped cubicle and rubbed her eyes and groaned. It wasn't even ten o'clock yet and already she was sick of being at work. The ennui, as she called it, had started for her about three weeks ago, a few days after her latest request for a transfer had been turned down. Instead of assigning her to the FBI's Behavioral Sciences Program for the coveted job as a profiler, as she had hoped, they had told her no postings were available. Then, convinced that it was what every woman wanted, they had given her a handsome young male trainee to shut her up.

The FBI top brass didn't know it, but Denise had found out through the grapevine that two men she knew from the Phoenix Field Office had indeed been assigned to the positions that supposedly weren't available. Neither one of them possessed a masters in Criminal Psychology, as she did. Neither one had done as well on the test. Both had less time in than Denise's twelve years. In fact, the sole qualification that had earned them the post rather than Denise was the usual one: they had penises.

It was around this time that Denise's work began to suffer. She was beginning to realize that she was going to spend her entire career in the "temporary posting" they had given her right out of Quantico, a job checking the serial numbers on circulating cash to determine if the money had recently been involved in bank robberies. It had taken her a few months of looking around at her co-workers to realize that this was a career graveyard, the place where the FBI sent their least best and least bright, the Siberia of the New York Office. Denise spent most of her first year convinced that it was a training period for her, getting her accustomed to FBI procedure. The second and third years she spent replaying every moment of her training in her head, wondering who she had pissed off. Then she decided she had just been forgotten about, and started filing transfer requests.

And now she had just resigned herself to the fact that the FBI treated women like shit. It was an old boys' club and she was never going anywhere and it was eight more years until she got a government pension – then she could take that and teach psychology somewhere. Actually use the master's degree, because it wasn't ever going to get any use around here.

Dick Yancey stuck his head into her cubicle. "Morning," he said. He was holding his ever-present coffee cup in one hand and waving a handful of files with the other. "Just got something."

Dick Yancey was the only person in her department Denise would willingly spend time with outside of work, primarily because he was every bit as sick of the FBI as she was. A fifty-eight-year-old Vietnam vet with a drinking problem, he had one year to go until retirement, and when he wasn't pulling sick days, he was sitting in his cubicle drinking coffee, staring at his screensaver with bleary red eyes. He was prone to going off on long monologues about the good old days, which made him the butt of jokes all around the office, but Denise often found a moral or some good advice in his stories, some of which she had put to practical use. Still, despite her respect for the man, it was his transfer to her department that had served as Denise's wake-up call that her job assignment was a ticket to nowhere.

She patted the bare corner of her desk, motioning for him to sit. "Whatcha got?"

Dick Yancey sat on the desk, put his coffee down, and opened a file. "It seems a bank in a town named Wilford, New Jersey got robbed on Friday. Five guys, all parolees. Locals got four of them. A statie shot the fifth at a gas station, but he got away."

"Oooh, violence."

"And plenty of it." Dick Yancey plopped the first file down on her desk.

"So, a fugitive. Do we know who he is?"

"That we do. I talked to the locals, then ran him for

everything on the database. He's had quite a career."
He plopped the second file down.

It wasn't even ten yet and already Dick Yancey had been working this case, collecting three files' worth of information. Denise had noticed before that Dick, who had a reputation for lobotomized laziness, would, on occasion, become diligent and aggressive if he was the first person to happen on a case. And he always handed the good ones off to her, rather than finish it.

She opened the file. "Philip Turner Dixon. Born 1964, Texline, Texas." She flipped past a few pages, the fingerprints and the personal info, and looked at the arrest record, whistled at the length of it. "This guy doesn't like to stay out of trouble, does he?"

"The locals think he had his own plan. He didn't have much confidence in his partners. Seems he planned all along to steal the bank manager's car as a getaway vehicle and he left out the back door."

Denise was looking at one of Dixon's psychological evaluations from a prison in Texas. "Says here he's above average intelligence."

"There are about five of those that say that."

"So we're dealing with some kind of criminal genius here?"

Dick Yancey laughed and held up the thick file of information on Dixon. "I wouldn't go that far. If he was a genius we wouldn't have all this."

"So how did we wind up with this?"

"Now to the good part." Dick Yancey held up the third file. "A Flying J truck stop in Kansas turned over its deposits to a bank on Sunday night, and they did a random check on the bills. One of the bills was from the robbery."

Denise tapped a pen against her chin thoughtfully. "Kansas. That would be on the way back to Texas, wouldn't it? You think Dixon's going home?"

"It gets better. A travel agent in a town called Tiburn, New Hampshire, called the locals on Monday, yesterday, because a woman bought a plane ticket with hundred dollar bills that appeared to have blood on them. They were from the robbery, too."

"So we've got the bills turning up in New Hampshire and Kansas. Weird. What do you think?"

Yancey shrugged, sighed. "I dunno. That's why I gave it to you. I'm going to knock off early today. Dental appointment."

Dick Yancey's dental appointments were famous all over the office. If he really had as many dental appointments as he claimed, he would have more teeth than an alligator, each one capped and polished. Denise nodded, suppressing a smile. "OK. Me and Wonder Boy'll take care of it."

"Why don't you go up to New Hampshire? Get out of the city for a few days? On the taxpayer."

"With Wonder Boy? I don't think so." If Denise went on an investigation, she was supposed to take her young trainee with her. Being alone in a car with him for a six-hour drive each way was not her idea of a vacation.

Dick Yancey winked. "I think he's got a crush on you."

Denise rolled her eyes. "Thanks for the case, Dick."

"Have fun with it. Take a break. New Hampshire's beautiful this time of year."

Denise detected a trace of concern in his voice. "Why? What's up?"

Dick shrugged. "You just haven't been yourself lately. I think you need . . . you know, a trip or something. Maybe a little excitement."

"Great. You think I need to go and spend some time with Wonder Boy in a motel in New Hampshire?"

Dick Yancey shrugged. "Hey, whatever works. You just seem kind of down, lately, that's all."

Denise smiled at him, squeezed his hand. "Thanks, Dick." She held up the file. "We've got this, you go to the dentist."

Denise had a lot of nicknames for her trainee, but the only one that didn't contain the word "fucking" was Wonder Boy, which was why she used it around the office. If spoken with the correct tone, it actually could be interpreted as a compliment, rather than the derisive put-down that Denise intended, and it was in this manner she found she could insult any number of her co-workers to their faces with a reciprocated smile.

Wonder Boy, or Agent Kohl, as everyone else called him, was a pleasant and intelligent young man who was going to shoot up the ladder of success at the FBI because he was gifted with charm, patience, an excellent resume and a penis. Denise, who lacked only one of those career attributes, would be working for him before her eight years to retirement were up, she knew. For this reason she was occasionally pleasant to him, on those days where she still imagined herself an FBI agent eight years in the future, but such days were getting scarcer with each passing month.

"What've you got going on, Denise?" Agent Carver, the squad supervisor, asked her as he leaned back in his chair, his head touching the wall in the cramped little conference room. Denise hated New York City offices, with everybody pressed up against each other and the conference table barely large enough to accommodate the opened files of six agents discussing their cases. She bumped Wonder Boy's elbows as she tried to find Dixon's file. If she'd gotten her transfer, it would have been the last time she'd ever have to deal with the elbow bumping and the squeezing past people in the narrow halls. More than just a change of assignment, she needed an office with some freakin' space. Even the trainee agents in Phoenix had offices with doors.

As usual, Carver discussed her case last, as if it were the least significant. Now everyone else's work was put to rest we could find out what Little Denise has been up to. And what was up with Carver calling her Denise? Everyone else in the room was Agent this-or-that. She decided, as she was pulling Dixon's sheet out of his file, that maybe Dick Yancey had been right. Maybe she did need to get out of the city for a few days. "We've got a fugitive from a robbery in South Jersey who is turning up bills in New Hampshire and Kansas," she said. "One Philip Turner Dixon. Lifetime criminal, armed and dangerous, and so on."

"New Hampshire and Kansas," Carver said. "They're not next to each other."

"No, sir, they're not."

"How'd he manage that?"

"My theory," said Denise, as if she'd researched Dixon thoroughly, rather than listened to Dick Yancey talk about him for five minutes, "is that he's in New Hampshire. I think he handed the money off to a truck driver who was going west, to spread the bills out and deaden the scent a little."

"That's pretty sharp," said Carver, shaking his head. "I doubt one of those garden variety broad-daylight robbery guys would have the sense to do that."

"This guy's been robbing banks since the eighties," Denise said. "I've got Corrections info on him from several different prisons which have scored him very high on intelligence tests." She pulled out a piece of paper and handed it across the table to Carver. "He seems to be the valedictorian of the Falstaff Correctional Facility. He also had a getaway plan from the bank robbery itself that worked. Everyone else in the robbery got shot or apprehended."

Carver looked briefly at the paper and shrugged. "Did you contact the New Hampshire locals?"

"Actually, I was thinking it would be a good idea to go up there myself." She waited a few seconds to let the statement settle. Carver was famous for letting his agents do all their work from their desks, hated the budget and paperwork nightmare of actually sending his agents out to do something. And when he did send people on assignments, it was always his favorites, Walker and Toney, his golfing buddies, the two guys flanking him at the conference table. Denise hadn't been out of the office in years. "It'd be a good experience for . . . Agent Kohl," she added, "an opportunity to get a little field work."

Carver winced. "I don't know, Denise," he said. "This guy's armed and dangerous." Apparently aware that he might have been overtly sexist, he added, "I don't want to lose an agent . . . any agent . . . over something the locals could handle."

Denise's brain was whirring, trying to think of a way to insult Carver to his face in such a manner that the insult would go over his head, when Kohl eagerly broke in.

"I think it would be an excellent opportunity to get involved with a field investigation, sir," he said. "I mean, I think my training would be more effective if I got a chance to get some hands-on work."

Carver nodded thoughtfully, now acknowledging only the young trainee. "You might be right, Agent Kohl. This might kill two birds with one stone. We could get you out into the field for a few days. OK, that's settled." He tapped the table, adjourning the meeting, and as he stood up, he said to Kohl, "Have Leslie draw up the paperwork and let's send you guys out into the field."

Dixon started awake because it was so quiet. After nine years at Falstaff and three months in the halfway house, he found it eerie sleeping in a house so still. He was used to the clanging of metal as guards slammed heavy steel doors and yelled short, clipped phrases to one another. "Block D check." "Open gate four." The shrieks of a late-night beating. After time, these rituals had become associated with sleep, as calming as the ocean.

The only noises he could hear in the darkness of Elias White's chilly basement were an occasional grunt and whir as the refrigerator kicked to life in the kitchen above him, and sometimes the faint dripping of the kitchen faucet when Elias failed to shut it off completely before he left for work. But today even those noises were absent. Dixon sat in the cot for a few moments and listened to the silence.

It would be like this when he bought himself a farm in Edmonton, Alberta, he thought. Silent. He needed to get used to silence, to normalcy. Maybe there'd be cows mooing in the fields, or chickens squawking, or alpacas making whatever noise alpacas made. They were all the rage now, in farming, supposedly. Their fur sold for a bundle. Fat Bill Guyerson had talked a lot about alpacas, before he had squealed on his mobster buddies and joined Witness Protection. Screw it. He was going with chickens. He didn't want to start out with heavy cattle; too much work and too little profit. Maybe some layer chickens to start, and see how that went. He'd wait to get cattle and alpacas, perhaps a few years.

He sat up, careful not to bump his head on the low alcove ceiling, and was surprised by how little the wound hurt. Those painkillers were sure doing their job. The nurse had given him three bottles of them, warned him never to take more than two pills at a time. She had been particularly unimpressed by the severity of the wound, which Dixon had found encouraging. "Have me come all the way out here for this little scratch," she had scoffed playfully. Scratch or not, she had taken the five grand.

"Don't spend it for at least a week," Dixon had warned.

"Don't worry, man," she had said, and Dixon had liked the way she said "man" not like an American, who just tossed off the word as if it was meaningless. From her, it meant she was acknowledging he was a human being.

She had done an excellent job of cleaning and wrapping the wound, and while she was working, Dixon had sensed that she missed treating injuries such as his, and was bored with her easy work at the college. By the time she left, leaving him with all the disinfectants and tubes and Latex gloves, the little alcove looked and smelled like an emergency room at a neighborhood clinic.

Through a tiny crack in the floorboards above him Dixon could see a sliver of light, and knew that it was daytime. From the silence, he figured that Elias had already gone to work. He groaned, rubbed his eyes, hopped off the cot and clambered up the basement stairs into the kitchen.

In the refrigerator, Dixon found a packet of sausages, which he had told Elias to buy the day before. There were two new cartons of eggs, and bags upon bags of cheese. For the last two days he had done nothing except sleep, drink water and cook a huge cheese omelet with a side of sausages. Then he'd wolf them down, and, patting his full belly, stare out the window for a few hours at

Elias's backyard, then stumble back down the stairs to his dark alcove and fall asleep again.

Today was Wednesday, Dixon figured. He and Elias had been housemates for five days already. Since Elias had gone to the college and summoned the nurse, they had hardly seen each other, because Dixon had been whacked out on painkillers and recovering from his injury. But today, as he tossed some sausages in the frying pan, he was starting to feel a little bit better. Some of his energy was returning, the pain was lessening, the bleeding had stopped. He felt confident that in another week, as he had promised, he would be able to get the hell out of here, head for the Canadian border, and leave this weird little pussy hound of a professor behind forever.

After he had scoffed down his meal, he looked out the window at Elias's backyard, admiring the tranquility of the scene. A neighborhood cat was off in the distance, looking up at a squirrel in the tree where Dixon had nearly passed out the night he first came here. It was like a painting. He wondered if Elias appreciated the life he had, decided probably not. People like him were always pushing, manipulating, trying to get something better, never grateful for what they had.

Suddenly bored, Dixon decided to wander around the house. He went up the stairs, something he had never done since the night he had surprised Elias in his bedroom. He peered into the same bedroom, where the sun was gleaming across the unmade bed, a book opened, face down, on the bedside table. Dixon went into the room and looked at the book. It was about a thousand pages long, and called *The Rise and Fall of the Weimar Republic*. He turned it over, flipped a page or two, trying to find something in it he might relate to. Just a lot of German names. He shrugged and put the book back exactly as he had found it.

In the next room, which Elias clearly used as a study, there was a computer, a desk and papers scattered everywhere. On top of a pile of bills was a manuscript, perhaps sixty pages, entitled *Was Hitler Right? An Analysis of Personal Records From the Second World War.* Was Hitler Right? What the fuck was this? This was the type of shit the Aryan Brotherhood fuckers would read in the joint, only there'd be bigger print and more pictures.

Then he noticed the words "by Elias White." So Elias was a Nazi. He didn't seem like a Nazi – all the Nazis Dixon had known had shaved heads, muscles and tattoos – but you could never tell. What the hell was a college professor doing writing shit like this? Dixon pulled up the office chair next to the computer, sat down, and began to read the great works of Professor Elias White.

6

"Look at those," Denise said, pointing out an area full of rhododendrons in full bloom. Since they had arrived in Tiburn a half hour ago, Denise had found herself smitten with the place, with its quaint New England charm and small-town atmosphere. Agent Kohl, as she had expected, couldn't give a shit.

"Yeah, they're nice," Agent Kohl said, his voice flat and his eyes trained on a young woman leaving the Tiburn Post Office across the street. "Why don't we pull over and ask someone where this travel agency is?"

Agent Kohl, despite his charm and good looks and fine résumé, was a flatliner when it came to personality. During the six-hour drive from New York City to Tiburn, Denise had tried any number of times to start a conversation she might care about. Every attempt fell flat. They did discuss, in great depth, the poor condition of I-278 (they REALLY should fix this road!), the astonishing number of toll booths in Connecticut (are the I-95 tolls the only source of revenue in this state?!) and the greatest conversational topic of them all, the weather (I think it might rain . . . Why do you say that?). Denise's one enjoyment from the ride was derived from the fact that she had worn a really short skirt, just to torment him, and had caught him looking at her legs at least three times in Rhode Island alone.

The one time Agent Kohl had started a conversation which had some promise was just after they crossed over into Connecticut, when he turned to her after twenty minutes of silence and said, "Lupo . . . is that an Italian name?"

"Yeah. My dad was from South Philly."

"What does it mean?"

"Wolf."

"So your name is Denise Wolf."

"No . . . it's Denise Lupo."

Five more minutes of silence, and Denise said, "Is Kohl German?"

"Yeah."

"What does it mean?" Denise asked, even though six years of high-school German had already given her the answer.

"I don't know," Agent Kohl said.

Denise knew he was lying. Who, at some point, hadn't become interested in the origins of their own last name? "I think it means cabbage," she said.

Agent Kohl said nothing. "Kohl, as in coleslaw," she continued, rubbing it in, knowing that a last name meaning "wolf" was cool and a last name meaning "cabbage" wasn't. "Kohl-slau. Slavic cabbage. That's where it comes from."

"Oh," said Agent Kohl.

Twenty more minutes of silence.

Denise was aware, as she looked at Tiburn's beautiful town square, that she was having one of her life's seminal moments. She was staring at the rhododendrons and the people and enjoying the simplicity of the moment. An elderly man was walking his dog and yanking its collar as it tried to piss on the Civil-War-era artillery piece in the middle of the square. A mother was reading a paper on a bench while her two kindergarten-age twin sons appeared to be strangling each other a few feet away. Feeling a warm glow, she looked across the street, where she noticed a sign saying "Tiburn Travel" on one of the shops down the block.

"Do you already know where this travel agency is?" asked Agent Kohl, almost sarcastically.

Denise pulled into a parking space and shut off the engine. "Don't you think this is a beautiful town?" she asked.

"Yes, it's very nice. But it's almost five o'clock, and we should find this place so we can talk to the travel agent who made the police report," Kohl said, as if patiently explaining something to a child.

Denise wished she were with Dick Yancey instead of this annoying kid. Dick Yancey would just want to go and find a bar and get shitfaced and deal with business tomorrow. That would be fun. Of course, Carver would never let her and Yancey go on a field investigation together. The only way she could even get out of the office was to take Wonder Boy along, and now she was paying the price. The seminal moment continued.

The seminal moment was Denise's realization that she was going to quit her job. This twerp in the passenger seat wasn't exactly the final straw – the final straw had been the last transfer application getting rejected – but he was the catalyst. Why couldn't he take five minutes out of his life and look at rhododendrons in full bloom and just appreciate the fact that he was out of NYC for a day? Fuck the FBI, and fuck Wonder Boy and his great résumé and his bright future.

"The travel agency is over there," she said, letting weariness and misery show in her voice. She got out of the car, locked and slammed the door and started crossing the street. She heard Kohl getting out of the car behind her.

"How do you know your way around this place?" she heard him calling after her.

"Attention to detail," she called back over her shoulder. "Something you need to learn."

When Elias came home from work, he knew the second he walked in the door that Dixon had been up from

110

the basement. Years of living alone in his own space had developed in him the unconscious expectation that none of his possessions would ever be moved by anyone except himself. He stood in the entrance hall for a few seconds and tried to determine exactly what it was that didn't seem right. The desk, the coat rack, the umbrella stand, all where they normally were. Why the impression of another presence in the house?

The mail.

The mail had been dropped through the door slot the usual way, but one letter had separated from the rest of them and was at an angle to the pile. It was as if someone had gone through the mail and tried to make it look like they hadn't. Someone. Whoever could that be? Elias picked the bundle of letters up off the floor and noticed immediately that the separated letter had a German postmark. It was from Ann.

He tossed his briefcase on a kitchen chair and got a bottle of wine from the cupboard, opened it, and sat down at the table. He looked at the letter, felt the thickness, turned it over in his hand. A white envelope. Normally an expressive woman, Ann would have picked a colored envelope for happy news. And it was thin and light. Whatever Ann had to say didn't take long. Elias already knew what was in it. He had known for a long time, but it actually being here changed everything.

He put the unopened letter in the middle of the table and went through the rest of the mail: his auto insurance bill, an offer for a free oil change at a new garage in town, a flyer from a local dry cleaner. He threw it all in the middle of the table with Ann's letter and poured himself a glass of wine.

Where was Melissa Covington when you needed her? She hadn't been heard from since last Friday, the day of Dixon's arrival, which was just as well. With a wounded bank robber in his basement, Elias was not enthusiastic about the idea of entertaining. But the girl had no idea Dixon was there. Had she just decided to end it? Had she found someone better? Her lacrosse coach, maybe? What made him, an up-and-coming young college professor, so easy to abandon? He looked at Ann's letter, and paranoid thoughts began to dart through his mind. Had Melissa come over, and Dixon had gotten rid of her? Or maybe she and Dixon . . . No, he couldn't, not in his condition. Elias was seized by the sudden desire to drive down to West Tiburn High and see if she was still at lacrosse practice.

He heard the stairs creak. Not the basement stairs, but the stairs leading to the second floor. As the rhythmic thump of a descent began, Elias became furious that Dixon had wandered around his house. What the hell was he doing up there? Hadn't the agreement been that he would stay in the basement?

112

Dixon walked into the kitchen, and Elias was further aggravated to notice that he was wearing one of his hand-knit sweaters. Without blood pouring from his side and dirt all over him, he looked surprisingly collegiate.

"What were you doing upstairs?" Elias asked, trying not to sound annoyed. Best not to pick a fight with a man capable of, and well-versed in, violence.

"I was reading." While Elias watched, Dixon began rooting through his cupboards until he found a glass. He sat down at the kitchen table, pointed to the wine bottle, and said, "You mind?"

Elias was surprised by the display of manners. He imagined, if Dixon had wanted some wine, he would have just taken it. Elias shrugged. "Help yourself."

Dixon poured himself a few gulps into the glass, which was in fact an old rocks glass Elias hadn't used in years.

"I can get you a wine glass," Elias offered.

Dixon took a long pull of the wine like he was an athlete drinking water after a sprint. "What's the difference?"

"It breathes better," Elias said.

"I don't mean what's the difference. I mean who gives a fuck. I just want to catch a buzz." He finished his glass and refilled it.

"It's not good for you, seeing as how you've lost so much blood. The nurse said you should reload on fluids. Wine's a diuretic. Plus, you're taking painkillers."

Dixon took a smaller pull this time, exhaled mightily, then put the glass on the table. "Damn," he said. "I haven't been drunk in nine fucking years."

"Why not?"

Dixon laughed. "Why do you think?"

"I don't know."

"Well, think about it. Where are there a lot of people who don't get drunk?"

Elias shrugged. "I don't know. A Muslim country?"

Dixon laughed again, this one cut short by a pain from the side. "I've been in jail, dipshit. Falstaff Medium Security Correctional Facility. Fourteen years for armed robbery, they let me out in nine." Dixon smiled. "Good behavior."

Elias didn't know what to say. "I didn't know that. I mean, I knew you'd robbed banks, but I never knew you'd been caught."

"Everybody gets caught."

"Why do you do it, then?"

Dixon poured himself another glass, emptying the bottle. Elias felt that Dixon had been asked this question many times before, and he was sizing him up, trying to best determine which of his many answers was most appropriate for a strait-laced college professor.

"Why do I rob banks? Hell, that's not a question. The question is, why doesn't everyone else? What's the matter with fuckers like you that all the bank robbery

114

is left up to people like me? Why don't you guys ever help out?"

Apparently it was the attempt-at-comedy answer. Elias would rather have heard one of the others. "Us guys?"

"You know, middle-class so-called normal people. Why don't y'all try it, once a lifetime. It's not hard."

Elias didn't feel Dixon was taking the conversation seriously, and attempted to end it. "You can't just go around robbing banks. Soon, there wouldn't be any banks," he said.

"Why would that be a problem?" Dixon eyed him across the table, and Elias had the feeling he needed to be careful, that this sociopath was about to get passionate. Best just to agree with everything he said. Oh, wow, yes, I never thought of it before, a bank robbery attempt should be a rite of passage for all young men.

"It would be chaos, the wild west," he said patiently.

"What do you know about banks?"

Elias shrugged. "I have an account."

Dixon pulled a stack of crisp hundreds out of his pocket, peeled off the top bill, and handed it to Elias.

"Look at that bill."

Elias looked at it. "Yeah? It's a fresh one hundred dollar bill."

"Where did it come from?" Dixon's eyes were alive with passion now, and Elias was watching his answers.

Elias studied the bill for a moment, looking for an indication of the mint, like there were on coins. He didn't see one. "The mint?"

"There are four mints, did you know that? Philadelphia, San Francisco, Denver and one in New York. Which one is that from?"

"I don't know."

Dixon took the bill back, held it up, and pointed to two signatures. "These two signatures. One's from the Secretary of the Treasury, one's from the Treasurer of the United States. What's the difference?"

"I don't know. What?"

Dixon pointed to several small letters printed at various points on the bill. "What does this F mean? What does this mean here, this F23? Here it says FW. What does that mean?"

Elias shrugged.

"What does this mean here, Federal Reserve Note? How is that different from a US note? What does this Federal Reserve symbol mean? What is the Federal Reserve, and what does it do?" Dixon was looking feverish with excitement, and Elias was getting worried, fearing an outburst.

"What's your point?" he asked cautiously, trying to make the question sound as non-confrontational as possible.

"My point is, nobody knows. Nobody ever wonders

116

about any of this shit. I got this from a bank. It's fresh, it's new. Where did the bank get it?"

"From the mint, I would imagine."

"Why did the mint give them money?"

"The mint didn't *give* them money. They bought it."

"With what? Money? What would be the point of that?"

Elias furrowed his brow, trying not to look confused, which would fire Dixon up even more.

But Dixon sensed Elias's confusion and rapped his knuckles on the table with excitement. "That's right. Nobody knows. Nobody knows where money comes from or how it gets here. Nobody really knows a goddamned thing about the most important thing in their lives, money. Nobody ever wonders about it, either. The only thing anyone knows about money is that they don't got enough. The rest of it, they just *assume.*" Dixon spat out the word with disgust.

"They *assume* everything is fair, man. They *assume* the people in charge of shit know what they're doing, and care, and aren't just a bunch of greedy cocksuckers stealing all our shit. They *assume* nobody would put a guy in jail unless he'd done something wrong. But look, every fucking day there's some new DNA evidence getting some guy off, some guy who has rotted away for ten years on death row waiting for the injection, and bam, it turns out he didn't do it. And you know why he was there? Cause he didn't have any of this." Dixon held up the hundred. "That's the fucking crime, man."

Dixon took a deep breath and finished his wine, then continued in a softer voice. "Look, here's how it is, man. They *assume* the banks and the government do everything fair, but fuck, nobody knows. And me, I think there's something that ain't right going on. If the government can just print money and sell it to the banks, why is the government in debt to the banks? Can you explain that? Why does a group that prints and sells money, like you say, owe hundreds of billions of dollars to the groups that buy it? Ya ever wonder about that?

"Why are sixty million people in debt to the banks? Why do farmers in Texas keep losing their farms to the banks? This is the richest country in the world, right? So why do millions of people owe the banks more money than they're ever gonna earn? And nobody knows a fucking thing about where money comes from, or how it gets here, and why the banks have so much of it and nobody else has any."

Elias said nothing.

"Ain't nothing fair," Dixon said. "Y'all think it is, but it ain't." He sighed, got up from the table, rooted around in the pantry and found another bottle of wine. He picked up Elias's wine tool from the counter, looked at it as if it was an artifact from another culture, then handed both the tool and the bottle to Elias. "You do it. I can't figure this fucking thing out."

Elias opened another bottle of wine.

"And that," said Dixon, holding his glass up for a refill, "is why I rob banks."

Denise Lupo drove slowly down the street, checking the house numbers against the address she had copied down from the travel agent. Angelique Davenport, 166 Bay Lane.

"This is it," said Agent Kohl, as if Denise couldn't have found the address herself, as if she were unaware that even-numbered houses were on one side of the street and odd numbers on the other. What a relief to have him here. Without his helpful and frequent comments, Denise would probably just drive up and down the street, bewildered by all the numbers and houses. She parked outside a neat but small split-level on the peaceful street, taking care not to get in the way of the street hockey game that a group of junior high school kids were playing a few yards from the car.

Kohl opened the door as if to get out, and Denise grabbed his arm. "Wait a second," she said.

"What's up?"

"Get yourself prepared. Have your weapon handy. There's a good possibility Dixon is in this house."

She thought she saw alarm flash across Kohl's face for a second, then he nodded. "Yeah," he said, as if he'd already thought of that. "I'm ready."

"OK, let's go." They walked up the garden path, and Denise took in the pleasant suburban scene. She needed a life more like this and less like the one she had. She was tired of her one-bedroom apartment on West 45th Street, wanted to see trees, have a garden. She liked the noise of children playing in the street. At thirty-six, she was starting to realize that she really wasn't the hardened city girl, the role she had been playing for the last twelve years. They came to the door, and Denise motioned for him to knock as she stood off to one side.

Kohl knocked on the door. They could hear a television blasting. Denise reached under her suit jacket and unsnapped her holster.

"WHO DAT?" The voice from inside was male, gruff, and aggressive.

She and Kohl looked at each other. "Just knock again," she said.

"WHAT CHOO WANT?" The TV was still blaring and he could barely be heard above it.

There was a few seconds of silence. Finally Denise called out, "Mr Davenport? We'd like to talk to you for a few moments."

More silence. Then they heard a chain being put on the door and the lock being worked. The door opened a few inches and a huge black man wearing a stained white T-shirt and boxers peered out at Denise. He looked enraged.

"There ain't no Mr Davenport," he spat at her. "There's a Miss Davenport, but she gone. What you want?"

"Excuse me, sir," Denise said, aware that if this man produced a gun and began to shoot through the narrow opening, there was absolutely nothing she could do about it. She adopted her most non-threatening, maternal voice. "We'd like to ask you a few questions. Can we come in?"

He stared at her. His eyes were bleary and red, Denise noticed, and she got a whiff of alcohol on his breath. A strong whiff. Her eyes teared up and she tried not to gag as she took another step back from the door.

"Who you? You ain't friends of Angelique." He gave Denise a long, slow, appraisal, most of it concentrated on her legs, and his expression softened. She smiled at him. Ooh, yeah, baby, just what I'm looking for, a fat shitfaced bully in his stained underwear. For the first time since they had left New York, she was glad Kohl was here. That feeling ended abruptly.

"FBI," said Kohl firmly, flashing his badge. Denise winced as the man's expression turned hard again.

"FBI? What you fuckers want with me?"

"We don't want anything with you, sir, we want . . ."

SLAM.

121

Denise looked at the closed door and sighed, then turned to Kohl. "That was smart," she said.

"We have to tell him who we are if he asks."

Denise sighed and rubbed her forehead. "We could have told him after we got inside, you rocket scientist."

Kohl said nothing. Denise was about to turn to go when they heard the TV shut off, then the chain on the door being slid back. The door opened wide, and the man stood in front of them now with a complete change of demeanor, head hanging, shoulders sagging.

"Bitch left me," he said. "She split. I don't know where she went." He looked rueful. "She ain't comin' back."

"She left yesterday?" Denise asked, trying to sound sympathetic.

"Yeah. Why the FBI want to know about this?"

"Well, she bought a plane ticket to Kingston, Jamaica, and paid for it with bills stolen in a bank robbery on Friday. Would you know anything about that?"

"What? Huh? No, I don't know nothin' about dat. What the fuck, you think I robbed a fuckin' bank? Is that what this shit is about?"

"Have you ever seen this man before?" Denise opened the file and showed him Dixon's picture. The man looked at it for a second and shook his head.

"How do you know she's not coming back?" asked Denise.

"She left a note on the fridge."

"Could I see it?"

"It's on the fridge," he said.

"Could you get it for me?"

"What? The fridge?"

"The note," said Denise patiently.

"It's *on the fridge*," he said again. "Come in." He pointed at Denise. "Just you. You can look at the note, and then you gotta leave."

Kohl and Denise looked at each other, and she gave him a nod indicating it was OK. The man opened the door all the way and Denise went into the kitchen while the man went over to the couch and slumped down again. Next to him was a bottle of bourbon, half empty, sitting on a busted coffee table amid the aftermath of what had obviously been a temper tantrum. She looked around the kitchen. Two potted plants were broken on the floor, and on the refrigerator, written in lipstick, were the words "CHARLES GOODBYE AND GOOD RIDDANCE. GET A JOB!"

Denise looked around the kitchen as she heard the over-loud TV roar back to life. On the kitchen table was an opened letter addressed to Angelique Davenport, RN, with a return address logo of Tiburn College. Denise looked inside the envelope and saw a pay stub from which the check had been removed. She carefully eased the stub out of the envelope and looked at it.

Fourteen bucks an hour? She thought nurses made more than that. Also scattered across the table were several buds of marijuana and a few rolling papers. Without thinking, she grabbed two or three of them, a couple of the papers, and the pay stub, and put them all in her jacket pocket.

"Thanks for your time," she called to Charles as she went out, waving to him.

He grunted.

She closed the door behind her and she and Agent Kohl walked back to the car.

"Find anything?" Kohl asked.

"She was a nurse at the local college," Denise said. She handed Kohl the pay stub, careful not to let the marijuana buds spill out of her pocket.

"A nurse? How do you think she knew Dixon?"

"I don't think she did. Remember the police report? Dixon had been shot. They found blood in every car he stole after the robbery. His first priority after he got here was to find a nurse so she could clean out the wound. Obviously Dixon paid her well enough to get out of a rough living situation."

"So he knows somebody here or he wouldn't have come here."

Denise nodded. "And that somebody probably works at the college. So tomorrow, we spend the day interviewing people on the campus. Sound like a plan?"

Kohl nodded.

"Let's go get a couple of rooms at the motel."

They drove to the edge of town, where they had noticed a small motel when they had come in off the Interstate. Denise handled the booking of the rooms to make sure there were two of them.

"Here's your key," she said. "We're next-door neighbors." She waved at the parking lot and the truck stop across a field beyond. "I got us rooms with a view."

"Do you want to get some dinner?" Kohl asked hopefully. Since the interview with Angelique Davenport's ex, he had become friendlier, and had several times mentioned that it was getting near time to "relax". Denise had said nothing.

"Nah, I'm not hungry," Denise lied. She quickly decided she would rather spend her evening sitting on her bed eating vending machine potato chips out of a bag than spend anymore time with Kohl, who looked disappointed at her response. Perhaps, as Yancey had suggested, Kohl had set his sights on a nice romantic evening, sharing their souls over a bottle or two of wine in Tiburn's most romantic restaurant. Gaaak.

"You take the car. I'm gonna stay in."

"OK," he shrugged. "What time tomorrow?"

"Let's meet here at nine."

"Don't you think an earlier start would be good? Say, eight?" He was getting professional again now that his hopes of a wild evening had been rebuffed.

"If you want to go down to the college before anything is open and hang around for an hour, knock yourself out," said Denise, opening her motel room door.

"OK," said Kohl, looking sheepish, almost smiling. He was trying to charm her. Oh shit. What was wrong with men? The bitchier you were the more they took it as a challenge. Look, being bitchy means I don't like you, it doesn't mean I want you to try harder.

"G'night," she said sweetly, slamming the door. Ugh, she mumbled under her breath. She tossed the motel room key on the dresser and took her coat off as she heard the rumbling of a storm beginning outside. She took off her jacket and hung it on the lone wire hanger in the rickety closet and kicked her shoes off next to the bed. Then she peered carefully between the dusty curtains out into the parking lot, where she could see Agent Kohl getting his bags out of the trunk, looking dejected.

Denise got the marijuana buds out of her coat pocket and looked at them, then took a whiff. The dank, musty odor returned her to the halls of her high school in Upton, Minnesota. With the memory came the feelings of hope and excitement for her future, and the almost volcanic energy she had back then. She would get out of bed at five o'clock for her track team meetings on mornings so cold that the farmers she would see on her way to the track would be breaking ice off the well covers, and she had been excited about where she was going. She had drawn her energy from the thrill of the competition, the delight in being part of a team, and the friends she had made. She had been one of the slowest runners on the team, not a natural athlete, as her coach had kindly put it. But he had kept her on the team because of her attitude, which was always so positive and friendly. Well, she thought, as she broke the buds up into the rolling paper, those days are over.

She didn't know what she could have done differently. Be a housewife? She could have married any number of guys over the years, but her career had always come first, and the men had not been comfortable with that and moved on. Denise had been determined early on that she was not going to wind up like her mother, talking about all the dreams which had gone unfulfilled so she could be a good wife and mother. In high school and college, she had decided that her career, not motherhood, was going to make the world a better place. She struggled through a challenging scholarship program at the University of Minnesota, then another scholarship degree at Stanford, keeping her sights set on the goal of becoming an FBI profiler.

She was, it turned out, not a natural academic either. Her good grades in both programs were the result of endless hours in the library and frequent tutoring, and she realized early in her higher education that her small-town schooling was not putting her on a par with the more affluent kids competing for the same scholarships. But once again it was her attitude, her extracurricular activities and her perpetual smile, which had won over the judges and boards. And, of course, her sincerity as she described her bright future: busting child molesters and serial killers and using her training, her gifts (she *was* a natural at evaluating people) and her belief in the system to make the world a better place.

The day she had joined the FBI had been one of the proudest days of her life. Her mother had thrown her a party, and Denise had flown back from California to spend it with her family. It was the last time she had seen her parents together. Shortly after, her father had passed away from a massive heart attack, the result of forty years of road construction and after-work drinking – but not before he had been able to brag to all his friends that his daughter was an FBI agent. Her mother had also died soon after from a stroke, thankfully before Denise's disillusionment had begun. She, too, had passed away while bragging to the nurses about the career of her only child.

She was eight years from retirement now and the world was the same shithole she had been too naive to notice it had always been. She had busted people, sure, but very little training or personality analysis had been required. Mostly she just waited for them to start spending their stolen money, or for jealous neighbors to squeal on them. Bank robbers were not the same as child molesters. Almost none of them were clever, and over half were drug addicts. A majority of bank robberies were committed by desperate people who had stolen small amounts of money from the fantastically wealthy and well-insured, and who rarely had the sense not to brag about it to potential informants. If they weren't caught on camera, they were usually caught at an auto show or a high-end clothing store, flashing their new-found wealth while trying to buy things no one from their neighborhood would ever legally own.

So instead of seeing herself as a guardian of the people, Denise had come to see herself more as a government-employed night watchman whose sole duty was to prevent the FDIC, another branch of government, from having to make payouts. She had become a businesswoman whose responsibilities to the public were entirely financial. And when she did have actual face to face contact with the people she apprehended, usually at their trials, she felt more sympathy than pride.

Denise had at first suspected, then slowly begun to realize, that her gender was more of a career detriment than her charm, personality, and positive attitude were attributes. Gradually, those positive characteristics had begun to slip away, until the FBI had wound up with the person it deserved, a sullen and uninterested cynic who smoked pot stolen from suspects in hotel rooms charged to the government. Denise finished rolling the joint and admired it. She had retained that skill, at least. She went into the bathroom and opened the window, which provided a view of the dumpster, leaned her head out and looked around. It was clear. She kneeled on the toilet and, careful to keep the smoke from blowing into the bathroom, lit her first joint in eighteen years.

The feeling hit her quickly. She smoked the joint down to a nub, and as she flicked it out into the dumpster, she was grinning, her eyes shut, enjoying the wind and noise of the rainstorm which had just begun.

"It's gonna storm," said Dixon.

They were both drunk now, and night was falling, and the first raindrops were making a staccato drumming on the kitchen window. Dixon loved the rain, partly because there was so little of it where he had grown up. When he had heard it thrumming against the prison windows at night it was the only thing that made him feel free. He got up to open the window and had to steady himself, unaware of how much he had wrecked himself on two bottles of wine. His tolerance had dwindled away to nothing.

"Let's go onto the back porch," said Elias. He, too, had some minor problems with his balance. He opened the back door and was surprised by the strength of the wind, the type of weather which caused havoc in towns that weren't used to it. Tiburn had a long history of storms like this and everything was fastened down. It had been years since the power or cable had gone out.

Elias stepped out onto the porch, holding a fresh bottle of wine in one hand and his glass in the other, and slumped down into one of the padded deck chairs. Exhaustion was overtaking him. It had been a long day, a long week. Where the wine had made him tired, it had made Dixon excited, and he didn't think Dixon would understand if he said he wanted to go to bed. He dreaded the type of evening he would often spend with Ann and her friends, his eyelids growing as heavy as bricks while they chattered, animated, about a certain professor's moustache or the pointlessness of including some book or other in a reading syllabus. All Elias would be thinking about would be polite ways to excuse himself, wondering why he always lacked the energy of those around him. Perhaps, he thought, it was because he hated everything about his life.

Dixon stumbled out onto the porch. He was holding his big silver pistol. Oh, Christ, what now? Elias was suddenly irritable, not in the mood to be threatened by this expletive-spewing madman, and the wine was giving him a sense of familiarity with Dixon, making him brave. "Is it time to threaten me again?"

Dixon wordlessly handed him the gun. Elias looked down at it, noticed the slide was pulled all the way back and the bullets had been removed.

"A deal's a deal," Dixon said. "I'm gonna go for a walk," he said.

"In this weather?" Elias tried to hide his relief, both at the prospect of some privacy and at this new development. He had the gun. He instantly found himself wondering whether or not Dixon had another one, a smaller one, tucked into his sock. Didn't all the TV bad guys do that, tuck small guns into their socks? He looked down at Dixon's ankles, which didn't seem to be concealing anything.

"I love this weather," said Dixon, as he stumbled down the stairs and wandered off through the backyard.

Well, that was easy. This maniac was a less intrusive guest than Ann's friends. Perhaps Elias would invite him over one day when Ann came back. If she came back. That would be a fun evening, Dixon running around screaming "fuck" at everyone while they walked around with their wineglasses held high, pinkies extended, discussing the stunning revelations of Salinger's mistress or the latest issue of *LitReview Quarterly*. Elias suddenly remembered the letter on the table. He'd read it tomorrow. He was momentarily glad Dixon was here, had distracted him all evening. He wouldn't want to have gotten that letter alone, in a quiet, empty house. He filled his wine glass, finishing the bottle, and watched Dixon disappear into the night.

Dixon had complemented the wine with three Percocets, and was feeling no pain as he stumbled off into the darkness. He bumped into a fence and felt no pain, probably would have felt no pain if a jackhammer had been applied to his foot. Tonight would be a pain-free evening. He had no idea where he was going, didn't care; as long as nobody came with him he'd have an OK time.

He crossed a road and wandered down into the thicket of trees he had walked through the night he had first approached Elias's place. The rain began to come down in sheets, and he let it soak him, marveled at its power to overwhelm him, to be the focus of his thoughts, when he had so much on his mind.

He slumped under a tree and pulled a bottle of wine from under his shirt, Elias's last one. The guy wouldn't mind – he'd looked about toasted back there on the porch. Dixon could tell the guy didn't drink much. He was the type of guy who would get drunk with someone if he thought it would get him ahead in the world, like with an administrator at his college, or a senior professor, but mostly he'd rather just use it to get young girls hammered and see what would happen. There had to be a reason for doing things with this guy. Dixon imagined Elias felt the time they had spent drinking together had been largely wasted.

Not so with him. He had been without alcohol for so long that this evening was almost special. Now that he was alone, under a tree, with no one bothering him, it was definitely special. He pulled out the wine tool he had taken from the counter and used the blade to cut away the paper, as he had seen Elias do, then worked the metal into the cork. It took a minute or two of struggle, and he accidentally jabbed the blade into his finger and released a slow trickle of blood, but the Percocets made the wound feel warm and friendly. When the cork popped free, spilling wine onto the soaked sweater, Dixon chuckled. He leaned back under the tree, swigged heavily from the bottle of 1999 Gridleiu Merlot, and, while a powerful storm drenched him further, tried to imagine his farm in Edmonton, Alberta.

Probably wouldn't be too much sun up there, he figured. It wasn't going to be like Texas, with the girls walking around in shorts and fanning themselves on their porches and smiling at him, real friendly. Girls up there probably wore heavy coats year round, and had those cold ruddy faces like the girls in Jersey. It would take some getting used to. It suddenly occurred to him that in a week or two, Alberta was going to be a reality, no longer a cell-block daydream, and despite all the research he'd done, he'd never been there so didn't really know it.

"Farmland's cheap for a reason," Fat Bill Guyerson had told him. Guyerson was a fifty-year-old, bearded Canadian who had bilked some wealthy Texan widow out of millions, and they had caught him racing for the Oklahoma border in a Ferrari. Dixon knew Guyerson wasn't going to be in the cell block long. When they met, Guyerson had been mulling over the possibility of giving the local DA some information on his friends, who were running a mail fraud scam, in exchange for early release. You didn't mull something like that over for too long. The first time you saw a dude getting his head slammed in a door, or getting shoved down a flight of metal stairs for some real or imagined insult, the idea of selling any info you had started to look real good to you. You could deal with the issues of loyalty later. Right then you just had to get the fuck out of there.

Dixon had never had anything to sell, so for him, loyalty had never been an issue. He had never thought any less of the guys who bent over for the DA. If there was a way out, you took it, everyone knew that. And he had enjoyed talking to Guyerson during breaks on the metal lathe, because, like any good con man, Guyerson had little tidbits of information on every subject.

"Where's a good place to go if you've got a bag full of money?" he had asked Guyerson one day.

"My home town," Guyerson had said. "Just outside Edmonton, Alberta. That's where I was headed when the troopers pulled me over."

"What's so good about it?"

"Simple life up there. Real cheap farmland. You farm and mind your own business."

The only thing Dixon knew about farming was that everyone left farmers alone. It seemed like a good way to live, as no one was leaving him alone down here. When he was in, they would look up his ass to see if anything was hidden up there, and when he was out, they would check his piss with chemicals to see if anything was hidden in there.

"The thing about Alberta is, if you tell all your neighbors a fake name, after a while, it becomes your real name," Guyerson told him.

"I ain't much of a farmer."

"No big deal. Get an alpaca ranch. That's all the rage now. Everyone's getting an alpaca ranch. I was thinking about it, too."

Dixon imagined himself riding around his alpaca ranch, herding alpacas. "What's an alpaca?" he asked.

Guyerson laughed. "They make you money."

"Maybe I'll just stick to chickens and cows."

But the idea had been born. He had gone to the prison library and looked up every last detail about Alberta, had studied the worn Rand McNally map with the cigarette burns in it until his eyes were red-rimmed, had learned the names and populations of all the small towns from Athabasca to Vermilion. He knew the elevation of the Cheecham Hills and the Caribou Mountains, and the distance of all the towns to the US border, which he knew he would never cross again. At the time, he had a prison job for a corporation called Travel International, and on their website he was able to view photos of the region. It looked like a pretty but frigid wasteland, only slightly different from the baking hot wasteland where he had been born and raised. It was perfect.

Then he had looked in the 1952 *World Book Encyclopedia* and learned about alpacas, which seemed to be giant, hostile sheep. Their coats were valuable, but everything he read about them spelled trouble, including a warning that they like to spit and bite. Maybe he really would just stick to chickens and cows.

"Farmland's cheap for a reason," Guyerson had told him again, the day before he disappeared, whisked off by the COs, who came and got him with a discharge notice. Guyerson had become concerned that in Dixon's enthusiasm for Alberta, he might have created a monster. "It's cold up there," he had warned.

Dixon had waved him off.

Now Dixon sat underneath the tree, the rain drowning out other noises and all feeling. His dreams of the last five years were becoming a reality, complete with the problems and details of reality. In his prison daydream, he didn't have to worry about the fact that he was on his way to Canada without a heavy coat. Did they have coyotes up there? What kind of ID did you need for a Canadian driver's license? Could you drive a farm tractor without a license? How much did a tractor cost? Did he need a tractor, or should he just get a horse? What fake name should he pick? Phil would still be good, but Dixon, no way. He'd have to have the name ready. You couldn't pause and think when someone asked you your name. How about Turner? That had been his mother's maiden name. No, traceable. He'd have to make something up.

A slow, steady grin spread across his face, as he realized that, for the first time in his adult life, he was going to deal with problems that had nothing to do with prison.

Denise listened to the rain drumming on the roof of the musty hotel, as high as she had ever been, and became aware of a connection to the case, to Kohl, to all things human. She even had a sudden touch of fondness for Carver. She was filled with a sense of certainty that Dixon was in town, and she felt an obligation to Kohl to find him. They would find Dixon and she would see that Kohl got more than his share of the credit, and Kohl would shoot up the ladder, have a glorious career, and he would never forget her.

Denise decided she would be his mentor. She would teach him how to do a suspect interview, what signs to look for. She would be firm with him, but never overly critical or harsh, and she hoped a situation would present itself where she could prove her value, one instance where she could make a dramatic and lifelong impression. She imagined Dixon had disguised himself as a janitor at the college and she would be the first to notice him, and Kohl would be awed by her skills of observation.

She chuckled, embarrassed by her fantasy. Still daydreaming that the FBI would respect her, after all these years. Would she ever give up? There was still fight left in her, she decided. Her career wasn't over. She felt a rush of respect for herself, at not giving in, not resigning, not taking a teaching job somewhere. She wished she had someone she could talk to, a mentor of her own, a Dick Yancey who still cared. She needed a female friend at the Agency, she decided. Or she needed a male friend at the Agency. She needed some kind of personal contact other than Agent I-don't-know-I'm-a-cabbage Kohl.

Speak of the devil, Denise thought, as she heard the car pull up directly outside the window. The headlights shone through the thin, worn drapes, and the engine idled for a while, then shut off. The car door opened and closed, and there was a gentle knock at the door.

Oh shit. Kohl had seen her light on, and wanted to talk to her. The possibility that he wouldn't go straight to his room had never occurred to her. The small, musty room reeked of pot and Denise's eyes were probably as red as a bunny's. She hopped up from the bed in her bra and panties and said, "Just a minute."

"I didn't want to . . . wake you up," said Kohl, through the door, and he started to explain something, while Denise searched frantically around for something to cover herself, gave up, and wrapped a towel around her waist. Her hair was still a little damp from leaning out the bathroom window in the rain storm, so it was believable she had just gotten out of the shower. She opened the door a crack.

"What's up, Agent Kohl?" she asked. He was soaking wet. Good. This wasn't going to last long. She hoped that her calling him Agent Kohl, rather than using his first name, had set the right tone of professionalism. What was his first name?

"Hi," he said. "Sorry . . . I . . . just wanted to make sure you were all right. What with the storm and everything."

Denise was leaning behind the door, trying to look alert, and her left hand was hooked around the door as she peered out. She noticed, because of the odd focus of the marijuana, that Kohl was acutely aware of her fingers. She realized he was expecting, or hoping, that she would pull the door open.

140

"I'm fine," she said. Trying not to sound cold, she added, "thank you."

Kohl took a step back and leaned towards his room. "OK then," he said. "Good night."

"Good night," said Denise, softening her voice. Kohl turned back to his room, his shoes squelching. He must have got caught right in the middle of the downpour. "Agent Kohl?"

He turned around hopefully. "Yes?"

"I was wondering . . . what's your first name?"

His smile was genuine for once, not political. "Chris," he said.

"Good night, Chris."

Kohl said goodnight and she closed the door. Chris. She should have known that. Nice smile. She hopped back on the bed, suddenly, inexplicably pleased with herself, and began to flip channels with the TV muted, watching silent images flicker by.

7

The morning was so beautiful that Elias almost didn't acknowledge his screaming hangover. His head throbbed as if an elephant had sat on it while he slept, but a cup of coffee and three aspirin dulled the pain. The ride to work along tree-lined streets, with the leaves turning a hundred different shades of red and gold, almost rid him of it altogether.

Most days Elias had nothing good to say or think about Tiburn. He just wanted to escape it. The locals were either wary country folk or rich pretentious hippies from Boston or New York who thought that moving into the woods had placed them on a moral plane above the rest of humanity. A delicate balance existed between the two groups, which the newcomer hippies pictured as the harmony of nature, though Elias saw it more as the relationship between a parasite and its host. The wary country folk got to sell the city hippies furniture and arts-and-crafts crap at a phenomenal mark-up, and the hippies walked around glowing with pride that they had furnished their homes with "authentic" goods, a word which nearly made them achieve orgasms of pious consumerism. Their friends back in Boston bought fake shit at Crate and Barrel, but they got the real deal at Billick's – the store in which Elias had been caught shoplifting *Playboy*s when he was fourteen and had never set foot in since.

But sometimes the fall was different. The light fog that hung around the tops of the trees, and the chill in the air, with the occasional odor of burning leaves, reminded Elias of the one pleasant memory he could think of from his childhood. When he was in elementary school, his mother used to take him on walks through the woods near the house, and he would tell her about all the things he had done that day. He remembered describing his introduction to fractions, and discussing a short film they had seen about Japanese culture, where the custom of removing shoes upon entering a house had intrigued him. Then they would return to the house, which was warm and filled with the smells of dinner to come. She had been an excellent cook. Often she would make him a small batch of cookies while he continued to chatter.

Even though his mother was listening, Elias had noticed, in retrospect, a far-off and dreamy quality to her responses, as if she was imagining a totally different life. Which, it turned out, she was.

Often, as an adult, Elias remembered those days and wondered if his mother had been afflicted with some mental condition – maybe that explained why she had abandoned him? The note she had left on the kitchen table seemed so clearly rational. She had waited, she explained, for "her chance to leave" until Elias's twelfth birthday, which in many cultures was considered reaching manhood. Elias had researched the matter and couldn't find a single culture, not even among the goatherding nomads on the African plains, where twelve was considered manhood. Thirteen, in a few cases, but twelve never. Elias concluded that his mother had done the same research and merely subtracted a year out of desperation and impatience. As for her sanity, there was no firm conclusion, and given that adult life had likewise convinced him that there was a better life outside of Tiburn, he could hardly fault her for that.

Maybe there was some kind of genetic hardwiring that brought about the powerful urge to be somewhere else upon reaching a certain age. Maybe his ancestors had been some kind of nomadic tribe that was always seeking greener fields. Or maybe it was the house, which just became so horribly familiar and dull. These were the factors their restlessness had in common. Or maybe the fact that his mother had felt this way at his age was purely a coincidence.

He pulled into the faculty parking lot, clutched his head, and moaned. Time to go to work. Time to babble to kids who didn't care about events he hardly knew about himself. His job was to read some history, then describe what he had read to bored, rich teenagers, so they could supposedly get a job that didn't involve wearing a nametag. What a scam. If he was going to be involved in this scam, he wanted to be higher up on the food chain.

When he got home tonight, he would read Ann's letter. It was still on the kitchen table. He wondered what Dixon would think of the whole situation, his collection of letters of abandonment from women. Perhaps his new roomie would have some kind of brilliant prison wisdom on the whole affair. He seemed like he had thought a lot of things through.

"OK, here's how it works," said Denise, as Kohl pulled into the faculty parking lot. "We split up. We just don't have the time and resources to interview everyone on campus. We'll talk to a few people from the nurse's log, anyone who has been in the infirmary in the last few days. Then we randomly check a few names. Then we hang the fliers." She was going to order a sheaf of wanted posters bearing Dixon's name and mugshot, which would carefully leave out the armed and dangerous part to avoid causing panic across campus. These people weren't New Yorkers, Denise had reminded herself. The notion of a bank robber in their midst might actually cause concern here.

146

"Here's what you have to remember," she said as they got out of the car. "Anyone who knows something they don't want to divulge is going to engage you in conversation. It's exactly the opposite of what you'd expect. They want you to leave and stop questioning them, so there's a need there to appear like that's not the case. They'll keep you hanging around. People who really don't know anything will just tell you that and be done with you. So keep your eyes and ears open for babblers."

"Babblers?" Kohl was actually listening to her, she noticed.

"People who don't want you to leave with the impression that they want you to leave. Got it?"

Kohl nodded.

"We'll talk to ten or fifteen people each, see if anything comes up. I doubt we'll get lucky, but you never know. Ready?"

"Ready."

"Your first drop-by questioning." She smiled at Kohl, an almost genuine smile. "I'm so proud of you."

Kohl rolled his eyes.

"I'm looking for a Mr White." Elias heard a woman's voice from the history department entrance hall. He was leaning back in his chair after his first class, wishing the throbbing in his head would go away. As usual, the class had gone particularly well. They were always more lively when he was hung-over, a phenomenon he could not explain. Severe head pain and nausea made him better at his job. Perhaps it was because there were real, rather than theoretical, reasons to be sickened by his line of work.

"*Professor* White," he heard the department secretary say, "is dreadfully busy at the moment." Good for you, Alice. He had left clear instructions as he closed his office door that he was not available, no matter how dire the need. "I can take a message and have him give you a call."

"It's very important," he heard the woman say. And he knew. Instantly. This was about Dixon. Motherfucker, they had found him. Even before he heard Denise say the words "Federal Bureau of Investigation" and hunt for an ID badge, he had sat up straight in his chair, a bolt of adrenaline going through him. Fuck. He gripped his head tighter as the movement caused an especially evil and paralyzing pain to throb anew in his temple.

What had Dixon done last night that they had found him? How could they have possibly located him in the woods up here in New Hampshire? What did they know? Shit. Shit. Shit. He fumbled around with the papers on his desk and tried to make it look like he was reading something terribly important from which he was being distracted. One of his students, a pleasant but inattentive young man named Jeff, had given Elias a flyer for a frat party on Friday and recommended he come. It was the best he could come up with at short notice. So when Alice pushed his door open and looked into the cramped little office, the dreadfully busy Professor White was studying a yellow piece of paper with a caricature of a drunk student holding a frothy brew.

"Professor," she said cautiously. "There's someone here from the . . . the FBI."

"The FBI?" boomed Elias, not sure if he sounded jovial, as intended, or panicked. "Whatever could they want?" He wondered if his quickened breathing was obvious to Alice, tried to minimize his heightened senses, became aware of his hands. Were they flicking around nervously? Was he staring at the flyer too hard? He put the flyer down, then picked it up again, as if he had missed a crucial detail. "Tell them to come in," he said.

Elias was expecting the FBI woman to be officious-looking and aggressive, and was surprised when Denise walked in. She was small, maybe five foot two, with shoulder-length black hair and amused, sensitive eyes. Elias was smitten. He felt instantly comfortable, and he put the flyer back down. He made an effort to stand up and shake her hand, but she nodded, as if he should forgo the effort.

149

"Hello, Professor White," she said cheerfully. "I'm Agent Lupo, FBI." She eyed the flyer on his desk, and leaned over it for a second, studying the caricature. "That looks like fun."

"Yeah," Elias nodded, no longer fatally self-conscious. "I wouldn't miss it for the world." They both laughed. "Have a seat."

Denise remained standing. "No, I don't want to keep you long. I just have a couple of questions."

Not long. That was good. No, it was great. Elias leaned back in his chair. "Sure, about what?"

Denise took out a notepad. "Last Saturday, according to the gate monitor, you visited the campus?"

They were asking about that? Jesus, what had that nurse told them? The self-consciousness and the awareness of his hands returned. He made an effort to keep them still. He started formulating a lie in his head. Dixon was holding him hostage. Dixon was threatening to burn his house down. It wasn't his fault. Melissa had come on to him.

"Gate monitor?" Elias asked.

"Yeah. It's a device that records the license plates of all cars going through the faculty entrance. The security guards check the photos of the license plates periodically, so if there's one that isn't registered, they can have you towed."

Elias nodded thoughtfully. "Modern technology," he marveled.

150

Denise smiled. "Why did you come up here on a Saturday?"

"I had some extra work," he said, pointing to all the papers on his desk. He was tempted to say something else, start describing all his extra work, of which he had none, but she didn't know that, and he decided it was better just to stare at her expectantly. She was very pretty, in an aggressive, forthright way, not like Ann, who had an aura of intellectual pretense about her. Elias wondered how long she would be in town.

Denise nodded. "Do you know a woman named Angelique Davenport?"

"The nurse? Sure I know her. She gave me some shots last year. For flu. I hate getting the flu, so I . . ." Elias became aware that he was babbling, talking almost excitedly about his flu shots. Calm down. "Got shots," he trailed off.

"Mmmm hmm," said Denise. She looked around his office for a second. "I hate the flu too," she said.

"Why are you asking about Angelique?"

"Angelique? You were on a first-name basis?"

Elias threw up his hands, a gesture of exaggerated innocence. "You just told me her first name. Besides, everyone is on a first-name basis around here."

Denise laughed. "I'm just giving you a hard time." She stared at him for a second, seemingly amused, and Elias wondered if he was being toyed with or flirted with. She

151

fumbled with a file she was carrying, then extracted a piece of paper with a mugshot of a man on it, with prison numbers on a clipboard under his name: Philip Turner Dixon.

"Do you know this man? Have you ever seen him around?"

"No," said Elias quickly.

"Take a look at it for a second."

Elias stared at the photo, wondering exactly how long a completely innocent person would stare at a photo before denying they knew the person in it. "No," he said again, shaking his head.

"Well," Denise said, putting the picture back in the file. "Sorry to take up your time. Please give me a call if anything occurs to you." She handed Elias a business card, and pointed at the yellow flyer and said, with a mischievous smirk, "I'll let you get back to work."

Elias laughed, partly at her little joke, and partly out of relief that she was leaving. "You came all the way up here to ask about Angelique?"

Denise smiled at him again, but this time, Elias detected something, an instantaneous expression of victory, as if he had just given something away. Maybe it was in his imagination. Anyone getting questioned by the FBI was bound to be a little paranoid.

"We just like to know what's going on," Denise said breezily.

"How long are you in town for?"

Denise turned away from the door. "Probably leaving tomorrow." She shrugged. "I might send my partner back down and stay the weekend. It's a beautiful town you got here."

"Tiburn? You think so? This time of year it's not so bad." Elias grabbed a piece of memo paper off his desk with his letterhead and was pleased to notice his hands were steady. He quickly wrote his home phone number. Let no opportunity go to waste. He wrote "Elias" under the number, even though the letterhead clearly gave his name. He had ordered the letterhead memo pad the day he had been given a professorship, and now, three years later, had found his first good use for it. "Give me a call if you decide to stay the weekend," he said. "I'll show you around."

"Thanks," Denise said, popping the paper in the file with Dixon's photo. She could have at least put it in her pocket, separated it from her business papers. "See you around," she said.

Elias nodded, quickly searching for a pleasant, memorable way to say goodbye, something that would leave her thinking of him as she went about her rounds. "Take care," was the best he could come up with.

She nodded and was gone. When he heard her leave the outer office, he exhaled, long and hard. Alice knocked on the door.

"What's the FBI doing on campus?" she asked.

"They were asking me about the school nurse," he said. "I have no idea what that's about."

"Terrible isn't it," Alice said.

"What's terrible?"

"She just disappeared. No one's seen her for days."

"Really? I had no idea."

Alice shook her head. "I hope they find that man," she said as she came into the office and dropped off an appointment slip. "Terrible thing. Anyway, Jenny Hingston wanted to reschedule. She had an appointment at 10:30. Is one o'clock OK?"

"Yeah," Elias nodded. He took the slip and tossed it next to the flyer. His hangover was gone, he realized. Adrenaline. That was best cure of all.

Denise was at the lunch counter in the student cafeteria, waiting for her pizza slice to come out of the oven, reminiscing about her college days. She looked around, seeing all the characters she remembered. Over there, the disaffected youth, all wearing black, probably reading Sartre or Wittgenstein. A few tables over were the backwards hats and sandals boys with the sports pages open, discussing the merits of a certain running back. There were three girls behind her in line, dressed as if to go clubbing in New York City, talking about a guy in their Intro to Acting Class. "He's so hot," one was saying. There was screeching and giggling. Denise suppressed a smile.

"How'd it go?" Kohl was waiting for her at the end of the line. Had he not been wearing a suit and tie, he would have fit right in. He was only a year or two older than most of the kids.

"Interesting," Denise said. "How about you?"

"Not interesting. Just a lot of 'I don't knows' and 'I never heard of this or that'. And," he added, "no babblers. What was interesting?"

"I had a babbler," Denise said as she sat down, motioning for Kohl to do the same. "But I think he just wanted to get laid."

Kohl smiled. "A horny old professor?"

"He wasn't so old. Young guy. But he said one thing that kind of interested me."

"What was that?"

"He asked me if we'd come up here just to investigate the nurse."

Kohl shrugged. "Yeah? So?"

"He said 'up here'. Everyone else who asked me about why we were here said 'down here'. They assumed we'd come down from the office in Concord. This guy assumed we'd come from the south. New York City."

"Sounds like enough for a conviction right there," said Kohl absently, eyeing one of the well-dressed girls who had been behind Denise in line. Denise laughed.

Sometimes Kohl could be almost funny, when he wasn't taking himself so seriously. It was occurring to both of them that this trip to New Hampshire might not have been a great idea, that there was little chance of finding Dixon, that he could well be in the truck that had been speeding across Kansas. Or had been. Probably in Texas by now, probably home and safe, while two FBI agents sat in a college lunchroom in a New England college trying to piece together his whereabouts.

"Do you think he's here?" Kohl asked, sounding tired. There was disappointment mixed in there, too, like he had really been hoping to find a lead here, something more significant than a college professor using the wrong preposition. Denise imagined that, in a few years, he might become a decent agent. Maybe he would get transferred to the Profiler program. Maybe he would crack key cases, bust a serial killer who terrorized whole cities. Maybe he would have the career that Denise had once imagined. It wasn't really his fault that he would wind up getting the breaks she never had.

Denise shrugged. "You don't think him saying 'up here' was that significant?"

Kohl laughed. "Why would he assume New York City? Do you think he knows where each bureau branch is located?"

"He might have known where the robbery occurred. New Jersey. Down there. So we came up here."

Kohl laughed again. So did she. She threw up her hands. "It's more than what you got."

"I'm gonna get a sandwich," he said.

"Hey Dick, it's me. Denise." She was leaning back in the rickety chair in her motel room, her cellphone on the table, her earpiece in, as she rolled another joint. It was two in the afternoon, and she had been thinking about getting high again the whole time she had been in the lunchroom with Kohl, the whole time she had been interviewing people at the college. Denise had kept suggesting they go back to the hotel to "regroup", as she put it, though Kohl had kept coming up with bizarre suggestions: let's do this, let's do that. Let's go stake out the nurse's house. Why? So they could watch her abandoned boyfriend stumble around drunk? Let's re-interview the travel agent. Maybe there was something we missed. He was a good kid, a little too enthusiastic. Raised on television.

"How are you, honey?" She found Dick Yancey's voice strangely comforting. She didn't have to be the adult with Dick. Training people, even a sharp kid like Kohl, took a certain mindset, a certain patience, which she was aware she lacked. She twisted the joint tight and held it up, admiring its sleek uniform shape. This was going to be a good one.

"I'm good. How are things back at the office?"

"Full of bullshit."

Denise laughed. "I need a favor."

"Sure thing. But I've got an appointment with the oral surgeon later . . ."

"This won't take long."

"Go ahead . . . what do you need?"

"I've got a guy I want you to run a check on. See if he's got a file." She paused while Dick Yancey gathered pen and paper, put the joint in the corner of her mouth, held up the lighter she had bought when she and Kohl had been getting coffee that morning in the convenience store.

"Go ahead," Dick said.

"Elias White." She spelled his name. "He's a professor here at Tiburn College. See if we've got anything on him."

"Will do. What's the story on this guy?"

"Just a possible," Denise said breezily. "Nothing serious."

"Possible what?" asked Dick with a snicker. Damn. How had he known something was up? "Possible date for this evening?"

"Dick!" Denise laughed. "No, he's a possible suspect. See if you can find anything that might connect him to Dixon."

"What does he look like?" asked Dick Yancey, not letting it go. She gave in.

"OK . . . he asked me out. Sort of. But he *is* a suspect. There's just something not right about him."

"I'll look into it, honey," Dick Yancey said. "Have a little fun up there." She was about to protest again when the phone went dead. She looked at the freshly rolled joint in her hand, kicked off her shoes, propped her feet on the cheap, pressboard end table, and fired it up. Damn, was she really that transparent? Maybe Dick just knew her too well.

8

. . . and which ultimately have left German people as the victims of one of the greatest propaganda movements in the modern media.

Dixon put the masterwork of Elias White down on the table and looked at it. It wasn't thick enough to be a book. Maybe it was a pamphlet. A pamphlet for the White Aryan movement, full of big words, trying to convince people that their points of view were the opinions of men of science. If you said something the right way, everyone figured you were smart. Not too many people had the hang of it, though. A lot of people Dixon had known came off like they were putting on airs. It was always easy to spot. "I purchased" instead of "I bought". "I adore" instead of "I like". The last time he'd had sex was with a woman who purchased things, adored things, and ate "supper". One of the things she'd adored, apparently, was black men, judging by the two mulatto kids running around her wreck of a house, for whom she had purchased supper with WIC coupons.

Dixon looked around Elias's study, wondering if there was more Nazi paraphernalia lying around. How deep into this shit was this guy? Maybe he was the head of some weird organization. The baldies who handed out leaflets in the joint had to get the leaflets from somewhere. They didn't write that shit themselves. But Elias's writing wasn't the type of shit you saw on the prison Aryan Nation pamphlets. It contained words like "synergy" and "paradigm", and it was nearly sixty pages long. He shrugged. He didn't want to know. He didn't care what Elias was into. Sex with high school girls, Nazi shit – and why the hell didn't he open the letter from that chick in Germany?

Dixon coughed and noticed the pain in his ribs wasn't as severe as it had been the day before. He was healing up well. But each day, as he started to feel better and notice his mobility improving, he found himself getting increasingly bored. He was no stranger to boredom. Boredom in prison had been so severe it was like physical pain. But he hadn't anticipated experiencing it when he was free.

He turned on the computer.

Dixon had spent four of his months in Falstaff in their supposedly educational Right to Work program, sitting in a chair in the only carpeted room in the entire prison. The carpet was there to deaden sound. There was something comforting about the carpet, as if being in that room, even for only six hours a day, carried some kind of status. He would field calls from people trying to find cheap hotel reservations, and he earned forty cents an hour, which was a nickel more than they paid the guys who made license plates. Being literate had its advantages, as did being white.

"You've been *specially* selected," the company flack had explained, as if some powerful bond now existed between them. "We've reviewed your record and we think you'd be a good fit for the computer room."

Here's where I give him the sign, where I acknowledge that I'm special, Dixon had thought. Dixon knew that this man, this ferrety-faced college graduate with a veneer of self-confidence, had never said those words to a black man. Here's where I wink and nod. Give the special handshake. The real reason this man didn't want blacks working in the computer room was because they *sounded* black. They had accents. Travel International didn't want a voice like that on the phone. But Dixon's southern drawl was slight enough to be considered unobtrusive, even charming.

It was cool with him. He was always picking shards of metal out of his hands in the machine shop, even when he wore gloves. Sometimes, he picked them out of his face, right near his eyes. If he could sit in one of these chairs and just chat with people for a nickel more an hour, it was cool.

They had taught him how to type, and to use the web, though the only sites that weren't restricted were the ones directly related to Travel International. He had a headset, and two men from the office would listen in to his conversations with the clients, making sure he obeyed the thick book of rules. The most important rule was to never let the people you were talking to know you were in a prison. "It's company policy that we don't give out that information," he was supposed to say, if anyone inquired about the whereabouts of the office. Giving their credit card numbers to convicted criminals might upset them. But TI was determined to give a second chance to America's unwanted, especially if they were working for forty cents an hour.

Three months into his dream job, Dixon had been having a conversation with a woman from Kentucky who inquired about his accent, and he had mentioned he was from Texas. She asked what town, and just as Dixon was about to say "Texline" the phone had gone dead. Dixon looked up to see one of the corporate men in the glass booth overlooking the room shaking his head.

"You can't give out personal information of any kind," he said. "That's your first warning. There won't be another one."

Then, about a month later, a woman had called to complain about one of Travel International's services. She and her family had apparently been offered a free vacation stay in some Caribbean hot spot, but every morning a salesman would visit them and pester them about buying a timeshare. Before any trigger from his brain arrived to stop it, Dixon said casually, "These people are a bunch of fucking snakes." The line went dead.

Back to the machine shop.

That would have been OK. The machine shop was hard physical work, but there was no glass booth. But a note from the TI people appeared in his report at his next parole hearing, and was the sole cause of his rejection.

"You still seem to have issues with authority," they had told him. Apart from that one incident, his last eighteen months had been clear sailing. Not even a harsh word with any of the other prisoners. One time he had even prevented a fight in the weight room by stepping in and talking rationally to two men he barely knew. That wasn't in the record. But a comment he made to a woman over the phone was justification for keeping him incarcerated for another six months.

And shortly after getting out, he had robbed a bank. Six months, ten years, ten thousand years. It's not like he was going to suddenly start liking them one day.

The computer fired to life, and, out of habit, Dixon went to the Travel International website. He admired some pictures of sandy beaches and young couples enjoying margaritas with a view of a tropical sunset. He stared at them for a few minutes, and no other use for this device came to mind. He shrugged and turned the computer off.

165

He went downstairs and cracked open the last of the beers. He wished he could call Elias at work and remind him to bring home another six pack, but no phones. That was the rule. He was good with rules. The ones he made for himself, anyway. They were the only ones that ever did him anything but harm.

Jenny Hingston wanted to be a history professor. Jenny Hingston was going to go to graduate school for history after she graduated, and Elias's class was very important to her. Very. She said the last word breathily.

Jenny Hingston had the legs for modeling and the cunning for politics, as well as the bloodline to run Hingston Motors, the largest luxury dealership in Concord, and there was no fucking way she was going to impoverish herself by hanging out with a bunch of eggheads who sat around talking about moral corruption in the Weimar Republic. But Elias enjoyed the deception. Most of his C students who desperately needed better grades just shamelessly begged. Jenny Hingston had taken the time to wear a short skirt and expensive perfume and lie to him in a voice which most men only heard in strip clubs and on phone sex lines. Elias's position on the whole grade improvement scenario wasn't that she needed to study – although that would help – but that if she expected him to wipe clean a semester's worth of apathy with the stroke of a pen, she was going to have to do more than dress up and talk in a breathy voice.

"Or maybe I'll apply to the FBI," she said, her voice still breathy, letting him know that giving her a bad grade might be a major mistake, not only for him, but for the future of America, which was depending on this graduating class for recruits for their protection against terrorism and serial killers.

A light went on, and Elias nodded thoughtfully. "I know an FBI agent," he said. "Maybe you should talk to her."

Jenny nodded, almost surprised at having her own random, whimsical view of her future taken seriously.

"I'm meeting her for a drink tomorrow night. She's an experienced investigator. Perhaps you should join us." This would be perfect. He now had an opportunity to ask Denise out, using the smokescreen of advancement in the knowledge of the nation's youth, while simultaneously arranging an innocent tryst with Jenny. Then, while buying them both drinks for an hour or two, he could decide, stress-free, which of them would be the more convenient bedmate.

"I'd love to," Jenny said. "That would be so cool."

"Give me your cellphone number," Elias said, offhand. "I'll give you a call tomorrow afternoon."

Jenny Hingston tore a piece of paper off Elias's pad and wrote her phone number down, with the name

"Jenny" written underneath in large, swirling, feminine script. She handed it to him, and he took it with a faraway look, perhaps even gazing at the clock on the wall.

"I'll call you," he said distantly.

"How do you know this FBI agent?"

Good question. How do you answer that one? She showed up this morning to ask random questions about a felon who's living in my house? "She's just in town right now," he said breezily.

"Wow. That's so cool. I've never met an FBI agent before." Jenny was wide-eyed, staring at him almost with adoration. He was the kind of guy who knew FBI agents, not just a dork who talked about the rise of National Socialism in pre-war Germany.

"Yeah, well, I'll call you."

"Talk to you tomorrow." She pulled a $200 pair of sunglasses out of her Gucci handbag and put them on, giving him a little smile and wave as she let the door shut gently behind her.

Oh, he was so in.

For an hour or two after Denise had first visited, Elias had been in a sweat. He had taught a class just before lunch, and let the students go early because he had been so distracted. Over and over, he imagined the scene when he got home and told Dixon the FBI were in town, and every time he pictured the scene, Dixon would become unstable. Dixon would beat him to death in his kitchen with a rolling pin, screaming about how Elias must have said something to someone. Or Dixon would calmly turn around and stab him with a filet knife, saying "I knew I couldn't trust you" as Elias slid quietly to the floor. As none of the scenarios ended with Elias alive, he came to the conclusion that it was best not to tell Dixon anything.

Which is why he was so surprised when a calm and conversational Dixon met him in the kitchen as he walked in with two shopping bags, and said, "The FBI are probably going to visit you soon."

Careful of a trap, Elias asked innocently, "Why do you say that?"

"Figure that bitch has started spendin' the money by now."

Elias started taking the groceries out of the bag and putting them in the fridge, noting that Dixon seemed to have changed. He was obviously feeling better. Color had returned to his face, and the sweaters from Elias's closet he had taken to wearing almost made him look like he could fit into polite society. Until he opened his mouth.

"But you told her not to," Elias said. "I was there."

Dixon laughed. "If she listened to that, she'd be the first bitch ever listened to me 'bout anything." He peered into the shopping bag and found the six pack.

He pulled one out and put the rest in the fridge, making a toast motion, thanking Elias, as he twisted the cap off and took the first swig. "Alls I'm sayin' is, get your story straight. The money guys'll come up if she starts spraying those bills around."

"Money guys?"

"FBI's got a department that tracks bills around. FBI, Treasury, I dunno. Some government fucks. They'll be up here eventually."

Elias had to respect the man. He really did know his trade. "Why do you think they'll talk to me?"

"They might have some record you visited the nurse. Maybe surveillance cameras around the college, something like that. Maybe the nurse kept a log, who knows. Maybe they got nothin'. Fact is, you never know till they knock on your door. So be ready with some bullshit, just in case."

Elias nodded. "Thanks for the advice."

"That's if they even get as far as the nurse. They'll probably just notice the bills in town, at a post office or a bank or something. Sometimes they do random checks. The nurse seemed like a cool customer, though. I'm sure she'll have some bullshit ready. Just make sure you do, too. You can't be too careful."

Elias nodded.

"Don't talk too much if they start asking you questions. They look for that. Just be real easy and cool."

"OK." Elias tried to recreate the scene with Denise, wondered if he'd talked too much, or if he'd been easy and cool. He wondered if letting an FBI agent know you were attracted to her was a bad thing. "What if it's a woman?"

Dixon froze. "What do you mean?"

"I mean, if the FBI agent who . . ."

"You motherfucker," said Dixon in awe, shaking his head.

"What?"

"They came today, didn't they? It was a fuckin' woman. And you tried to get into her pants."

Elias said nothing. Was this guy psychic? He started to shake his head and Dixon stopped him, half concerned but also half amused.

"You fuckin' little pussy hound, can't you control yourself for five fuckin' minutes? Do you know what they're gonna do to you if they find me in your house? This is serious shit here. This ain't like gettin' a bad grade or something. You're gonna do time. Hard time. A scrawny fucker like you is gonna get traded around the cell block for a pack of Newports, you know what I'm sayin'?"

"All right, calm down."

"I'm calm." He was, too. He was looking at Elias, now clearly amused. "Well, the FBI ain't here, so obviously you did OK."

171

"It wasn't like that." Elias said. "She just asked some questions."

"I know what it was like." Dixon took another swig of his beer. "If you fuck her, don't bring her back here."

"I have some common sense," Elias said.

"No you don't."

Elias got red-faced, feeling a flush of anger and resentment, and Dixon noticed it and laughed.

"I'm just kiddin', man. You're all right."

Elias angrily put the frying pan on the stove, turned on the gas, and Dixon said, "She had her keys, you know."

"Who had her keys?"

"That kid next door. When she came over and told you she was locked out. I saw her let herself into her house with her keys. So she had 'em the whole time."

Elias said nothing.

"Alls I'm sayin' is, you gotta watch people. You gotta watch 'em the whole time." He took another swig of beer, then grabbed the six pack from the fridge and opened the door to the basement. "I'd better stay away from the windows. Tell me when dinner's ready."

"Do you know how hard it is to quit the FBI?" Denise asked. They were in a bar called The Raven, chosen not for its atmosphere or drink specials, but because it was about a hundred yards from their motel. Kohl was looking absently around, trying not to let Denise notice he was scoping out two college girls chatting in a booth by the bathrooms. They had been eyeing him, too, but had given up hope he was going to approach them – probably because they figured he was with his mother, Denise decided. She smiled to herself at the thought, and watched the college girls act as though they were involved in deep conversation.

But for the four of them, and two professional drunks mumbling to each other at the far end of the bar, the place was deserted. In two or three hours, the bartender assured them, it would be packed to the door with college kids from Tiburn, the ones who wanted to get off campus and were "real" enough to hang out with the townies. Because The Raven was also frequented by Tiburn's drunk and unemployed, the college kids considered it gritty, and becoming a regular there was a sign of maturity, demonstrating an ability to relate to people of all classes. The bartender told them that the novice drinkers, the freshmen with the fake IDs, rarely showed up here. How then, Denise wondered, to explain the acrid aroma of spilled beer and vomit which seemed permanently ingrained into the rough and aging woodwork?

"To quit? Why would I want to quit?" Kohl asked.

"I'm just asking if you know what is involved in the quitting process."

"No." Kohl looked confused. "Are *you* thinking of quitting?" He stared at her, and she realized that no answer she could give would surprise him. She wondered if there were behind-her-back conversations already going on in the office that Kohl might be privy to. Perhaps her resignation being tendered was an idea that had already been discussed.

"How long did it take you to get this job," Denise asked. "I mean, how many interviews did you have to go through?"

Kohl shrugged. "A lot."

"Did they send people to your house to interview your family and friends? Ask them whether you had used drugs in high school?"

"Well, yeah. That's not all they asked."

"No, of course not." Denise tried to smile warmly, aware that she might not be pulling it off. "But they interviewed your high school friends, didn't they?"

"Yeah. That's what they do. It's a government job. They do that to everybody."

Denise nodded and picked up her vodka tonic, pulled the last of it out from under the ice with a gurgling sound which alerted the bartender. She motioned for another.

"Two weeks' notice," she said. "That's all you have to give them."

Kohl nodded. "I'd never looked into it. I just got here, I haven't been planning to quit."

174

"They make you think you're special, that they need you. They act like you're a part of some elite, because you jumped through all the hoops to get hired. But you only have to give them two weeks' notice to leave. That's what I had to give at my last job waiting tables, before I joined the Bureau."

Kohl nodded again. He looked anxious, like he wanted her to stop talking, as if the conversation was making him doubt Denise's sanity. She might as well have been discussing her abduction by aliens. She smiled at him again, and this time it did come off warmly.

"Why don't you go chat with those two girls over there," she said. "They were looking at your ass when you came back from the bathroom."

Kohl looked over at the girls, then back at Denise, his face quizzically scrunched. "Are you OK?"

"I'm fine." She was surprised to see that Kohl seemed genuinely worried about her. "Thanks for asking."

"All this talk about quitting . . ."

"I'm just thinking out loud." Kohl didn't look satisfied with that explanation, and she laughed. "Look, Agent Kohl," she began.

"Chris."

"Look, Chris. I'm going to stay up here for the weekend. You can take the car back tomorrow and when you leave, drop me off at that car rental place."

He looked more confused and worried than ever.

"Carver's not going to expense you up here for the weekend, and he's definitely not going to expense a second car . . ."

Denise put her hand on his. "Look, honey," she said. "I just want to stay up here for a few days by myself. I like the town. It's like a vacation. I'm going to pay for it, OK?"

Kohl looked like his head was going to explode. What was wrong with him? Couldn't a girl just take a vacation if she felt like it?

"Do you have some lead on Dixon?" he asked. "You want to collar him by yourself?"

"Oh, Jesus," Denise groaned. She was about to smack him in the back of the head when her cellphone, which she had left sitting on the bar, rang.

"Hello?"

"Denise, it's Dick Yancey. How are you?"

"Fine, Dick. Me and Wonder Boy . . ." – she gave him a wink – "are sitting in a local watering hole catching up. How're your teeth?"

"My what? Oh, fine. Hey, I got that info you wanted."

"Yeah, go ahead."

"Elias White comes up clean. Nothing. Not even a parking ticket. And I couldn't find anything to connect him with Dixon. He seems to have lived his whole life in Tiburn, New Hampshire."

"His whole life?"

"Only one address. His address on his driver's license now is the same as the one when his father registered his birth certificate. I don't think he's ever moved."

"Wow. He sounds like quite an adventurer."

"There is one thing, though. His mother, a Janet White, is listed as an unsolved homicide in LA County in 1981."

"Unsolved homicide. That's sad. What was she doing in LA?"

"Couldn't tell you," said Dick. "Anyway, that's all I got."

"Thanks for calling."

"Sure thing. You have a good night."

She put the cellphone back down on the counter, and noticed Kohl looking at her suspiciously. "Was that about Dixon?"

"About the professor I spoke to today."

"You know where Dixon is, don't you? You're going to collar him yourself."

Denise laughed. Even as she laughed, she knew that if she were a man, she wouldn't be having this conversation. So much for being his mentor. Her male co-workers always viewed her with a measure of distrust, as if she was constantly planning something, always had an ulterior motive.

"Yeah, OK, you got me," she said, the light humor gone and her voice now tinged with a trace of bitterness which made Kohl flinch. "I just broke the case wide open, sitting here drinking vodka tonics. And now I want to send you home so I can arrest an armed felon by myself."

"We're partners, right? You can tell me what you know."

"*I don't know anything,*" Denise cried, with exasperation. "I just asked Dick Yancey to check on that professor I told you about, and he came up clean. That was all. I don't think Dixon is even in this town."

Kohl stared into his empty glass for a second. "I'm gonna go back to the motel," he said, clearly unconvinced.

"You don't want to talk to your girlies?"

Kohl shook his head as he walked out, not in response to the question, but to signify that Denise was a lost cause. "See ya tomorrow."

"Bye." Denise turned back to the bartender and pointed at her empty glass again.

An hour later, the place had filled up considerably, just as the bartender had promised. Most of the clientele were workmen who all seemed to know each other, and every one of them checked Denise out when they came to the bar to order drinks, but none spoke to her. Either way was fine with her. The vodka tonics were taking her on a cheerful ride through her own consciousness, at one point even convincing her that she was genuinely fond of Kohl. She had begun to ask herself probing questions about why she was even here; did she think there was any possibility Dixon might be in town, or had it just been a ruse to get back at the FBI, to force them to send her on a vacation because they obviously weren't sending her to Quantico to train for the Profiler program?

Ah, who knew? Maybe Dixon was here. How else to explain the nurse's disappearance and the bills showing up bloodstained at a travel agency? But maybe there were other ways to explain that. Even if the blood in the cars Dixon had stolen after the robbery matched the blood on the bills, what did that mean? All it really meant was that the *bills* had wound up here, and a nurse had left her boyfriend after acquiring them. She was getting lost in thought when she noticed a young man in a flannel shirt eyeing her across the bar. She looked away quickly, stared into her drink, as if suddenly fascinated by it.

He was in his late twenties, with friendly dark eyes and a pleasant smile, and he was next to Denise before she could decide how she was going to handle this. For a brief moment, she wished Kohl would come back in, begging forgiveness for his idiocy, but she knew from experience that waiting for her male co-workers to beg forgiveness for their idiocy was a long and thankless chore. Kohl was in bed and this guy was standing next to her now, waiting for the slight turn of her head which would mean she would have to acknowledge him.

"Hi," he said. "I'm Dave."

She nodded at him, careful to keep from being too friendly, and wondered if she should just say, "I'm leaving," and pay her tab and be gone. But Dave seemed like a friendly type, not excitable or weird in any way, and she wanted one last drink, and Denise decided he might turn out to be good company. "I'm De . . . Deborah," she said.

He offered his hand and she shook it, a big and powerful hand with thick, rough fingers. He had some dirt on him, but not much, and she figured that he was a construction worker, probably drywall, and most likely a supervisor. It was a game she liked to play, guessing people's jobs from a quick glance. "What do you do for a living, Dave?"

"I'm a supervisor for McCauley Builders," he said. He pointed sheepishly at his dirty sleeves. "Sorry about this. Me and the guys came here straight from the job. We just finished a project at the Merrimack Development. Hey, Paul!" Dave waved to the bartender and held up two fingers. "What are you drinking, Deborah?"

"Vodka tonic. Thank you." There was little choice but to stay now.

"What line of work are you in, Deborah?"

OK, that was annoying. Ending everything he said with

a mention of her name sounded a little car-salesman-like, as if he was trying to prove he could remember something for more than ten seconds. Especially as it wasn't even her name.

"I'm applying for a teaching position here at Tiburn College, *Dave*."

"Oh yeah? What field are you in?" He sounded genuinely interested, surprising her. She had figured she would get in three or four words about herself, then listen to the story of his life for the rest of the evening.

She started to have some guilt feelings about making up an entire alter ego, wondering how bad it would have been had she told the truth. You could never tell people you were an FBI agent, though, it was always the same shit. They were either way too impressed (wow! . . . the FBI, that's so cool!) or wanted to discuss exactly what had happened at Waco or Ruby Ridge, as if Denise's own errors of judgment were responsible for those episodes. Her Italian friends back in New York just laughed, and taunted her about taking ten years to convict John Gotti. So it was best just to be an unemployed professor looking for a job, she decided. "History," she said, remembering her visit to the history department.

Two of Dave's friends came over, both of them drunker and louder than Dave, but equally friendly. "Introduce us to your lady friend, dude," one said. He was a tall, thin, unshaven man with tattoos on both arms, and more dirt on him. Not a supervisor, Denise figured. Another guy behind him was young, barely twenty, and seemed to admire the tattooed one, looked to him for behavioral cues.

Dave made the introductions. The tattooed man took her hand and pronounced "Deborah" eloquently, and gave a slight bow, as if meeting royalty. She smiled. The younger guy, amused by his antics, shook her hand sheepishly and stepped back behind him, like a kid hiding behind his mother's legs.

"Dude," the tattooed guy said to Dave. "We're going to step outside and smoke."

"You guys go ahead," said Dave, turning back to Denise.

"You can smoke in here," said Denise, knowing exactly what they were talking about. She giggled, and the tattooed guy came around Dave and made a motion toward the door with his head, inviting her.

"Sure," she said.

Dave looked surprised. "Wow," he said. "You're a history teacher, and you get high? What about all those young, impressionable minds?"

"Where do you think I get the pot?" she laughed. She was having fun with her alter ego now, the bad history teacher who bought pot from her students, though she didn't think, after all the vodka tonics, she was up to inventing much more. Of course the truth, the bad

FBI agent who stole pot, was even worse, so she figured she was really coming pretty close to telling the truth. Truth, lies, whatever. She'd be back in New York, bored to death again, in a couple of days. "Have fun while you can," she said aloud, though she had only meant to think it.

"Amen to that," said the tattooed guy.

She followed them outside. They opened up the door on a pickup truck and let Denise sit in the passenger seat, legs out on the running board, and the tattooed guy handed her the packed bowl and a lighter. Dave pulled a six pack out of the back, and the four of them chatted for at least an hour, the bowl getting repacked time and again. They found her fake life story endlessly entertaining, and as the pot took hold of her, she found herself increasingly adept at telling tall tales. Mostly, she figured, they just liked meeting a stranger. Finally, giddy from all the vodka, beer, pot and attention, she announced it was time to go.

"I'll give you a ride home," Dave offered hopefully.

"No, thanks, I'm only right there." She pointed at the motel down the street.

"Nah, let me give you a ride."

"No, really, I can walk." Barely.

"She don't want your ass, man," the tattooed guy said to Dave, and he and the kid burst into peals of laughter. Dave just looked disappointed.

"Well, good night then," he said, sounding sad. For a brief moment, Denise thought about inviting him back. He had a nice way about him, was a good-looking guy. Nice hands. She liked hands. And she giggled as she thought of the look on Kohl's face in the morning when he saw a guy leaving her room . . . That would be worth it.

"Good night. Thanks guys," she said quickly and turned to go. She wandered off down the wide, quiet road, suddenly realizing how drunk and high she was. She could hear them talking about her; they were unaware of how well their voices carried in the cool, still, night air, or not caring. One of them began singing 'Hot for Teacher'. She giggled again, and nearly stumbled. As she made it back to her room, closing the motel room door behind her and tossing herself down onto the rickety springs of the aging bed, still in her clothes, she realized that for the first time in several months, she had actually had some fun.

When Elias got home, there was another letter from Ann. Again, plain white envelope. He groaned, but decided it was time to read them both. He opened the one from earlier in the week first.

Dear Elias, I think we both know that we've been growing apart lately . . .

Yeah, no shit. Maybe because you moved to another country, could that have anything to do with it?

. . . and I want you to know that I will always care for you . . .

What was that, a consolation prize? The notion of Eternal Love, just as long as you're not around? Christ, even her Dear John letters were copied from some kind of a formula. Elias imagined that she had been to a bookstore and found a text in the self-help section with a title such as *Unloading Your Boyfriend Gracefully*. Get to the point. You got picked up in a bar by some Aryan asshole and you've decided to go with him now because he is more inclined to impress your friends at parties. He skimmed down the letter.

I met someone . . . Peter . . . Peter . . . Peter and I have decided to move in together . . .

He skimmed further. Peter this, Peter that. Elias remembered he and Ann had gone out for drinks with a young, good-looking German doctoral student who had been in charge of the exchange students' orientation program, and seemed to recall that this fellow's name had been Peter. He wondered when, exactly, this plan had been hatched. Perhaps Ann had been thinking of unloading him and taking on Peter when Elias had gotten up to go to the bathroom. Even her first letter back from Germany had been breezy and distant, focusing more on neutral topics like schoolwork and the weather than any actual connection they had ever had between them. Elias guessed she had driven straight

185

back from the airport where she had watched his plane fly off to America, and gone out for drinks with Peter that very night, both of them relieved at last to be rid of him.

Elias tossed it into the middle of the kitchen table, opened a bottle of Spanish Merlot, and picked up Letter Two. Was this a change of heart? Had Peter dumped her? Why a second Dear John so quickly on top of the first?

This one started off nicely enough, with a plea for understanding, but then followed up with a request for Elias to mail her two books that she had stored in his attic. These were a dense six-hundred-page volume about the rise of the Hapsburgs, and a sixty-dollar coffee table book of Helmut Newton's nudes. A check for postage would be mailed immediately, if Elias asked for it, as well as the actual packing materials. The entire bottom third of the page was devoted to the exact location of the two books, in either the box marked "Books" or the one marked "Books and CDs". The letter ended with the suggestion, "If you could please try the one marked 'Books' first."

Love, Ann.

Love.

Elias had to laugh. Finally, it was over. Their façade of a relationship had mercifully closed itself out, not with the bang of a screaming match but with the whimper of a bitch begging for some expensive books she was too cheap to replace. Why these two books? He understood the need for the Hapsburg book, because she was working on a doctoral thesis on that very subject. But the Helmut Newton book? Was she really so pretentious that her new German apartment urgently needed the works of Helmut Newton displayed prominently on her coffee table? Well, yes, she was. Elias had always known that.

Elias went upstairs. He pulled down the retractable attic steps and looked up into the dusty, cramped and cobwebbed room, the stale smell of airlessness and mould overwhelming him as his head crossed the threshold. It was warmer up here, too, by at least ten degrees; the heat Elias was paying good money for was mostly trapped up in the rafters. He needed to talk to someone about insulation. He shined a flashlight around the room and saw some of Ann's boxes, and pulled them towards him. BOOKS. That was the one he was supposed to try first. He tossed the box down the attic steps, where it landed on the floor with a *thunk* violent enough to shake the whole house.

Elias carried the box downstairs to the kitchen, where he cut the tape with a knife. Though he and Ann had never lived together, he had permitted her to use his attic for storage while she was away, and he always figured that the extended connection they shared through his control of her things would serve to continue the relationship. Apparently, Ann was of the opinion that banging a German doctoral student didn't change anything with regard to the original storage agreement. It was this naiveté that Elias had found refreshing when he first met her, and which he now found laughable.

The Hapsburg book was on top. Elias took it out and looked at it, gently turning the pages of the old text, running his fingers over the gold embossed title, and he enjoyed the warm, rich smell of the leather binding. He tossed the book on the table. Against the edge of the box, stacked differently from the others because of its size, he found the Helmut Newton book, and he pulled it out. As he did so, a few papers fell out from between the pages and landed on the floor.

Well, lookee here. That must have been why she wanted the book, not for the marvelous photography but for the documents she had stored in it. One of the pieces of paper was her birth certificate. Another was her college diploma. Anne Phillips, Tiburn College, Class of 1998. Now, why would you be asking for your birth certificate when you lived in Germany? Had somebody lost their passport? Hee hee hee. He ripped the diploma and the birth certificate into pieces, then picked up the knife and stabbed the Hapsburg book. The knife went in far enough to stand up on its own. He stepped back to admire his handiwork, and then noticed Dixon in the basement doorway, looking at him.

"Dude, what are you doing?"

Elias said nothing. Dixon came out of the doorway, into the kitchen, and looked at the book with the knife wound.

"This is an expensive book," he said. He pulled the knife out and looked at it. "It was a minute ago, anyway."

"You want to read it?"

Dixon flipped through the pages. It was over 600 pages long and the print was tiny. "Doesn't look like my kind of thing." He picked up the photography book and opened that, and saw black-and-white nudes of some European models. "This, on the other hand . . ."

"Take it. It's yours."

Dixon took his eyes off the models for a second. "Why you want to get rid of this? It's a nice book."

"Just have it. Take it with you." Elias turned around and found his bottle of Merlot left open on the kitchen counter. He refilled his glass. "Want some?"

Dixon nodded. "Sure, why not." He flipped through some more pages, then noticed the torn papers all over the kitchen table. "What're these? Hey, this is someone's birth certificate."

Elias handed Dixon a glass of wine.

"You know," Dixon said, taking the wine with a nod of gratitude, a habit which impressed Elias – he had noticed that his basement felon, when he wanted to, had excellent manners – "I'm on the run from the law.

I really can't be carrying around a ten-pound book full of pictures of naked chicks."

"Bet it would stop a bullet next time you get in a shoot-out." Elias laughed, enjoying his own wit.

Dixon ignored him, turned the book over in his hands, and then noticed the price on the inside cover. "Jesus, sixty bucks for this? Why didn't you just buy a *Penthouse?*"

"That's Ahhhhhhht," said Elias, hoping his drawn-out syllable was a good impression of Ann at her most pretentious. Like when she would come home and start talking about various incidents in German history she had learned about, going out of her way to introduce certain historical characters whose names required specific pronunciations which she had practiced to perfection. He remembered how she had impressed that German dickhead Peter with her pronunciation of certain German words, and how she had given Elias a victorious little nod. There had been disagreements about that back in Tiburn. Elias would always wince when she started with her breathy 'ch' sound, which Elias just pronounced like a 'k'. *Kristallnacht,* she would purr, as opposed to Elias's "Crystal Knocked". Provincial little Tiburn just hadn't appreciated her.

"Hey," Dixon said, as if the idea had just suddenly occurred to him, though he had clearly been thinking about it for minutes. "I need a favor."

Elias paled. "What?"

Dixon let a moment pass, acted like he was still looking at the pictures of the nude models. He'd give Elias a chance to relax. Or to imagine the worst. Then when Dixon asked the favor, and it wasn't as bad as Elias had thought, there would be relief. Either way, it was the kind of thing said best after a pause.

"What? What? What?" snapped Elias. "What could you possibly want now? You want me to drive a getaway car for you when you knock over the post office? You gonna ask me to kill the FBI people? What?"

Dixon stared at him, a slight smile forming, still half-looking at the models. "Yeah, the getaway thing. That's what I was gonna ask you."

Elias sipped his wine and said, "Fuck you." Dixon laughed, because it was the type of thing which he should have said while swigging from a bottle, rather than while daintily sipping. This guy cracked him up. It seemed sometimes as if his daintiness was grafted on, and the graft hadn't taken well, and some core part of him was trying to reject it.

"I'm going to give you some money. I want you to spend it in a bar."

Elias looked at him quizzically. "And then what?"

"Then bring me the change."

"And?"

"That's it."

"That's it? Spend money in a bar then bring you the change?"

"Yeah. I'm heading off soon. A few days. I'm going to need a lot of twenties. All I have is hundreds and they draw attention. I want you to do it in a bar because bar money comes from everywhere. Goes everywhere. If they track the bills, which I doubt they will, that'll stop the trail."

"All right."

Dixon pulled two hundred dollar bills out of his pocket. "I'll need one twenty back. So I'm giving you eighty. Go have fun."

Elias nodded. "Thanks."

Dixon finished his wine with a gulp. "I'll let you get back to stabbing books."

9

Denise was lying on her bed in the motel room, looking at the ceiling, wondering if staying two extra days in Tiburn to relax had been a big mistake. For the last few days, when she was here with Kohl, she had been imagining all the beauty she would appreciate if only she could get rid of him, and have some time to herself. But now he was gone, having dropped her off at the car rental place that morning, and all she wanted to do was lie in her motel room and stare at the ceiling. It wasn't as much fun without Kohl to avoid.

Maybe it was the crippling hangover, she decided. Maybe tomorrow she would be filled with energy again, and would go exploring the parks and shops and restaurants of Tiburn with the enthusiasm she had imagined. But tomorrow was Sunday. What if everything was closed? And she had to be back in New York by Monday morning, so she would have to check out tomorrow morning. She groaned, and put her hand over her eyes, as even the light of the dim hotel bulb was causing her head to throb anew.

Her cellphone, lying on the pillow next to her, rang, and she groaned again.

"Hello?" she croaked.

"Is this Agent Lupo, with the FBI?" A man's voice.

Oh fuck. A business call. On a Saturday morning. She sat up stiffly and ran her hand through her hair, trying to adopt a professional posture which might make her sound more professional on the phone. "Yes, this is Agent Lupo." She saw herself in the mirror, a bedraggled hung-over mess.

"Hi. This is Elias . . . Elias White." There was a pause while the caller waited for the impact of his name to sink in, during which Denise tried to remember why the name sounded so familiar. "The history professor you spoke to yesterday," he added helpfully.

"Oh, yes, yes, Mr White. Hi." The horny professor who she had thought had been hiding something. And whose mother had been killed in LA.

"Doctor." He corrected quickly. "Hi. I wanted to know if you'd decided to stay in Tiburn for the weekend, or if you had headed back . . ."

Again, she had that fleeting suspicion this guy was hiding something. It was as if he had been about to say where she was heading back to, and had stopped himself, though she had never mentioned it to him. "No," Denise said. "I'm here in Tiburn. I think I might have made a mistake."

"Why's that?"

"I dunno. I'm wondering why I stayed." She was

surprised at herself for honestly divulging her sudden frustration to a stranger. "Should have gone back with my partner."

"Well, I have a proposition for you," Elias said. "I have a student who is very interested in joining the FBI, and I was hoping you could meet with us. Give her some advice, anecdotes, whatever. She'd find your input invaluable." There was a pause while Denise considered this, and Elias sweetened the pot with, "I'll buy you dinner."

"OK," said Denise, after a pause. What the hell? Her dance card wasn't exactly full, and a free dinner would be nice now that she had developed buyer's remorse over dropping two hundred on a rental car and a motel room. "Italian?"

"We can do Italian, but I know a great seafood place."

"Seafood's great, too."

Denise took down directions and they agreed on seven-thirty. She hung up and tossed the phone down on the bed. That was something to do, anyway. Might be interesting. How boring could a history professor be? Oh wait, that's right. But at least she'd get to talk to a guy who wasn't in the F B fucking I. And meet a hopeful, optimistic student who she imagined would be a mirror image of herself, a dozen years ago.

It took Denise about a third of a second to realize that Jenny Hingston was not a hopeful young version

195

of herself a dozen years ago, and that something else entirely was going on here. Jenny Hingston might one day be a rich man's wife, or maybe, if she opted to support herself, a socialite or a porn star, but one thing she was never going to be was an FBI agent. Not with a six-hundred-dollar Coach handbag and highlights that must have been at least half that.

That left the probability that Denise had been asked here not so Elias could try to screw her, as she had imagined, but as a device to impress one of his students, whom he clearly *was* trying to screw. Denise drew this impression from the body language between Jenny and Elias in the instant before they realized she was approaching them, and her brain processed it in the exact same third of a second when it was noticing that Jenny Hingston was a rich, attractive bubblehead.

"Hi," Denise said, beaming warmly, and they both turned and smiled at her, Elias awkwardly, as introductions were made. Jenny Hingston had excellent social skills and spoke in a low and breathy voice as she introduced herself. Too used to male attention, too poised for twenty-one or twenty-two. Denise wondered what she was getting out of this evening. An A, probably.

"We're waiting for a table," said Elias. "Can I get you something to drink?"

Well, fuck it. Some free vodka tonics might soften the blow. She was about to ask Elias for one when she realized, hey, if I'm getting dragged out here and made to play a part in their play for the evening about a young girl who wanted to be in the FBI, I'll get the good stuff. "Ketel One and Tonic," she said.

She remembered that that was how last night had started, with her having just one or two drinks at a bar, ending with her smoking pot in a truck with some plasterers while she regaled them with tales of a profession she had never even thought of entering. She wanted to cover her face at the memory, but she just smiled as she accepted the drink from Elias.

"Thank you, Professor White."

"Elias, please."

He paid for the drink with a hundred, and seemed to want her to notice him doing it. Funny, he didn't seem the flashy type. It was a weird gesture. Maybe he was tired of the myth that all professors were broke, and was trying to prove otherwise.

Denise turned to Jenny and said pleasantly, "So, I hear you're interested in a career in law enforcement."

"Yuh," said Jenny, staring blankly across the top of her drink, the sip straw still in her mouth.

Yuh. Denise contrasted that response with what she imagined her own would have been, twelve years ago. She would have loved to have gotten the insight and advice of a female field agent of twelve years' standing, would probably have prepared a list of questions to ask.

What are the key factors in the application process? How easy is it to transfer departments? And most important of all, how do they treat women? Is it really as progressive a work environment as they claim?

Yuh.

"I think it's cool," Jenny said, removing her face from the sip straw for a second, "that you're an FBI agent. I think that's so cool."

"Thanks," said Denise sweetly.

"Do you like, get to use your gun a lot? Do you ever shoot people?"

"Sure, I shoot people all the time. I just shot two people on the way over here."

Elias laughed extra hard to make sure Jenny understood it was a joke, and Jenny half-laughed with him, making the whole scene so strained that Denise decided to just be nice. "Now might not be a great time to join the FBI," she told Jenny.

"Why not?"

"It's very much a male-dominated field right now," Denise said.

Jenny shrugged. "I don't mind working with guys."

OK, this was going to be a long evening. The history professor had better offer up some interesting conversation quick, or she was going to bolt after the appetizer, remembering the . . . what? What excuse could she use when she was out of town? She had to go visit the police station to make sure they got flyers of Dixon. That would be a good one. To prepare them for it, Denise asked, "Where's the local police station from here?"

Elias gave her cursory directions, then asked why she needed them.

"I have to swing by there later to make sure they got flyers of the guy we're looking for."

"Flyers?" Elias seemed suddenly very interested in her job. It was not an uncommon reaction from men, but Elias's interest was disturbingly detailed. "Where will they hang flyers?"

"Wherever people might see them. The Post Office, for instance. Municipal offices, state or federal buildings. The cable company might run some info about him, depending on what kind of local access you have. We usually feed a picture to the local press, but I'm not sure it would be a good idea in this town."

"Why not?" asked Elias.

"Small-town people are easy to scare. This guy's violent, a long history of crimes with a weapon. So we'd need more solid evidence that he was actually in town."

"So you're not even sure he's in town?"

"No we're not." Denise looked at him with her most serious FBI face and said, "Why don't you tell me what you know?"

Elias gasped, choking on his drink. "I don't know a

thing," he protested, his voice high-pitched with the screech of innocence, the color draining from his face. By the time he realized that Denise had been joking he had already completely lost his composure, and Denise found it odd he was so jumpy. Perhaps the social stress of trying to screw one of his students was wearing on him.

"No, you got me," Elias said, having composed himself. "This guy's living in my basement."

"Ah-hah," Denise said victoriously, glad to have discussion of her work behind her. "Another mystery solved."

"You're like a modern-day hero," said Jenny Hingston, suddenly aware of being left out of the conversation. "I mean, like with September Eleventh and stuff."

September Eleventh and Stuff. Maybe that was the title of the Official Airhead's Guide to Terrorism. "No," Denise protested, her voice laced with the undetectable irony she had perfected. "The real modern-day heroes are people like your professor here."

Elias blushed, mistaking, as she intended, her insipid flattery for genuine praise. Oh, men were so dumb. But Jenny picked up on it and immediately began to regard Denise as a possible hostile presence in her midst.

Their table was called, and as they walked over to it, Denise was aware of Jenny giving her a complete physical appraisal, with an obviously critical eye meant to inspire insecurity. She's checking out my ass, Denise thought. This girl was good. She hadn't risen to the top of her sorority food chain by being a sweet airhead. Denise was surprised to notice that even from this dumb little bitch, it did inspire insecurity. But only for a second.

Oooh, this dinner might be fun after all.

As he handed the menu back to the waiter, Elias suddenly realized that he was expected to cover the entire bill. He couldn't very well expect Jenny to fork over any money, because she was his student, and you couldn't ask your students to chip in, it just wasn't cool. And he had asked Denise to come as a favor to him, so unless she pulled out an FBI expense card of some kind he was on the hook for the whole thing. He started the calculations in his head. Tilapia and a brie appetizer for Denise, a salmon salad for Jenny, and a roast duck for him, which he had ordered because it was the cheapest thing he could find on the menu that didn't sound cheap. The pulled pork entrée was also seventeen dollars, but he would be damned if he was paying that for something that sounded like it should be served at a picnic.

Elias knew he had Dixon's two hundred dollars, but Dixon had only given him eighty of it, as he wanted the rest for change. With the Tilapia, brie appetizer, salmon salad and duck, that was his eighty right there, if you included the drinks at the bar. Plus tip, plus more drinks they were going to have at the table . . .

"What are you thinking about? You looked stressed," said Denise, almost affectionately. She had seemed caustic and combative when she first walked in, with an unnerving habit of saying ambiguously hostile things with a sweet smile. But damn, Elias had to admit she looked good. Where Jenny was slim and perfectly turned out, her nails and hair groomed, her perfume subtle yet noticeable, Denise was curvy and simplified. A nice, professional beige skirt, showing a pair of what Elias thought were perfect legs, and a red shirt which hinted of ample breasts without resorting to showing cleavage, as Jenny had done.

But as soon as they had sat down to eat, the combativeness had disappeared. Maybe FBI agents really loved food, or maybe there had been some subtle shift in the dynamics of the relationships between the three of them. Elias sensed he had somehow become the focus of the two women, and they were about to have a contest with their flirting skills, which had been his plan all along.

"Now you've got a shit-eating grin," said Denise. "You're clearly somewhere else."

Elias snapped back into the moment. "So tell me about banks," he said. "How does the money go from the mint to the bank?"

"What?"

"I was having a conversation with a friend of mine recently, and he was suggesting that when mints print money, there is some kind of nefarious activity that goes on. How does the money get from the mint to the bank?"

"In an armored car, probably," ventured Denise.

"Does the bank pay the government for the money? And if so, why is the government in debt to the banks?"

Denise giggled. "I don't know. Why don't you ask the Chairman of the Federal Reserve? I'm an FBI field agent."

Elias nodded, took out Dixon's hundred and handed it to Denise. "What does this letter F here mean?"

"Well that I can tell you . . . It's a series indicator. But I don't think you'll get to the bottom of any conspiracy theories by knowing that," she said. She handed the bill back to Elias. "You . . . or should I say your friend . . . doesn't trust the government, does he?"

"I'm pretty certain my friend doesn't," said Elias. "I don't have an opinion about it one way or the other." They were looking at each other with an intensity that Elias was thoroughly enjoying, and Jenny, who suddenly realized she was going to be excluded from this conversation, announced she was going to the restroom.

"Are you sleeping with her?" Denise asked the second Jenny was out of earshot.

"No," said Elias. "Why do you ask?"

The brie appetizer arrived and Denise moved most of Jenny's accoutrements to the edge of the table so she and Elias had room to share it. "Why do I ask? Oh, please."

"What does 'oh please' mean?"

"She's your *student*," Denise said.

"And?"

Denise rolled her eyes, and they both dipped into the warm brie.

"So you're saying it would be unethical?" Elias asked.

"Do I really need to explain that?"

"No. You need to explain why. You know what most ethics are? They're an excuse for people to get up on their high horse and start crapping on each other. Most ethical restrictions on our behavior have no bearing on anything."

"What do you mean?"

"Well, take priests for instance. You know why it's considered unethical for priests to have sex?"

"Because chastity brings them closer to God."

Elias shook his head victoriously, getting exactly the answer he had hoped for, as he prepared to impart the one fact he still remembered from a course about the church in the Middle Ages. "Nope. It's because the church used to give the priests land, and if the priests didn't have heirs, the land would go back to the church when the priest died. You think all these priests with blue balls are any closer to God? No, they're sitting around thinking about getting laid all day, because that's what humans do. And they're getting those blue balls so the Pope can stay rich."

Denise shook her head in wonderment, smiling in a way which Elias didn't how to interpret: as enjoyment of the conversation or a mask for shock. He opted for the former. "How does that excuse you for sleeping with your students?"

"I'm not sleeping with any of my students, but what if I were? You think it would inhibit their learning? Look at her. You think she's going to be incorporating the lessons of Hindenburg's weak leadership into her life any time soon? You think she's intrigued by Hitler's rise to power, how a man who never got more than a third of Germany's vote became the supreme ruler of a democracy? No, of course not. She's going back to Concord to run her dad's car dealership, with a degree that's nothing more than window dressing. So why shouldn't I just fuck her brains out, because she's more likely to remember that three years from now than anything I tell her about the Reichstag fire."

Elias was surprised at his rant; not by the content, which was something he had always strongly felt, but by how much he sounded like Dixon. Fuck her brains out. Jesus, the guy was rubbing off on him. And he had been surprised by what a rush he had felt when he had handed Dixon's hundred dollar bill to Denise. Here you go, here's the entire case right in your hand. He had wanted to burst out laughing when she handed it back without really looking at it.

Denise now actually was laughing, something that hadn't seemed possible when they had first met. "You're awful," Denise said, but in a way that indicated she also found the awfulness intriguing. "If you know she's just going to go back to Concord to run her dad's car dealership, why did you want her to talk to me about being in the FBI?"

Elias realized it was time to make a decision here, to commit. The way the evening was developing, it looked like Denise was going to be the one. Maybe Jenny some other time. "It was an excuse to see you again," he said. "When you came into my office, I thought you were stunning. I couldn't stop thinking about you."

Dixon heard the car pull into the driveway as he lay on his makeshift cot in the pitch-black basement. All evening he had been listening to the sounds of the country, the occasional car going past, the wind rustling through the trees. It was a beautiful change from prison, where there was always a fluorescent light on and every sound echoed throughout the monstrous steel cave. There had always been the voices of other men, some angry, some conversational, but constant, until even beatings and screaming became white sound, a noise to drift off to sleep by. But here there was silence and wind and bird noises and the blackness of the basement, and even in the blackness Dixon knew where his beers were. He liked lying in the complete blackness, his sense of vision completely neutralized, because it made him think that death might not be that bad.

He heard Elias's car door open, then the passenger door opened and immediately he heard a woman's voice. The voice was clear and self-assured, not the voice of a young girl. Elias must have picked on someone his own age this time.

"I like your garden," the woman said, and Dixon liked the sound of her, felt a rush of envy that he would never meet her. He liked her because Elias's front garden was an open-air botanical mortuary. Elias muttered something about not having green fingers. Then Dixon heard a key in the lock.

They came inside, then there was silence, and Dixon thought they might be caught in some kind of passionate embrace. Then he heard footsteps as they came into the kitchen, directly above him.

"I've got wine and tequila," he heard Elias say, and he noticed Elias sounded excited, a little breathless, but controlling it. The tone of his voice reminded Dixon of a predatory cat eyeing some prey species on the African plains, like he had seen in nature documentaries in prison. The bastard had tequila? Where was it hidden?

"How about a shot of tequila, then a glass of wine," said the woman. She was in the living room now, and Dixon could hear her walking around thoughtfully. She must be looking at the pictures on the wall, noticing small things about the house to give her clues about the man. Women were always looking for clues. So was Dixon. It was a necessity for the hunted. This woman knew the recipe for a total loss of control, but she didn't have the rough voice or demeanor of an experienced drinker. Dixon figured she wanted to get drunk tonight, then fuck Elias and forget about him.

He heard a door slide open, and he knew it was the sliding cupboard over the washing machine. The bastard hid his tequila behind the detergent. Hid it from who? Himself? It must have been there for a while, since before Dixon showed up. There was the sound of fumbling for glasses, and the opening and closing of doors. Then the distinct sound of pouring, and Elias went into the living room, where the voices were giggly and more muffled.

Elias said something muffled, and the woman said something back. Something that clearly sounded like "FBI". Dixon froze in his cot, now listening to the conversation intensely. Glasses clinked together, and he realized the muffled comments had been toasts prior to downing the tequila. Elias had said something about history. The woman had said something about the FBI.

That brain-dead, death-wishing motherfucker had brought the FBI agent back here.

10

Denise lay in bed looking at the cracks of light coming in through Elias's blinds, her mind whirring. She was comfortable under the covers but her head hurt and she knew she wasn't getting back to sleep, not with Elias kicking around. She had become used to sleeping alone, and though she didn't always love the alone part, she had to admit the sleep was better.

It must be about seven, dawn already, she thought. Oh God, I'm not drinking again for a long time. This is two mornings in a row now I have woken up with a pounding in my skull. I am going to pickle my liver like Uncle Mike. Coffee would be good. Aaaah, coffee. Maybe a tall cup of fresh coffee will make the skull pain stop. Or maybe it will just give me an acid stomach to accompany the pain.

She wondered if Elias had a cafetière. He seemed like a cafetière kind of guy.

Elias's legs thrashed again and then went still. What was up with that? It was like he was having dreams about being a soccer player. He didn't snore, but he did mumble, and when he had woken Denise in the middle of the night, mumbling, her first feeling was a rush of sympathy, as she imagined he was reliving the day he found out about his mother's death. It was the only fact she knew about him, and it gave her a protective feeling towards him. She could attribute any aspect of his behavior to it, from the fact that he seemed to have no moral center, and an ability to justify anything he did with rehearsed history lessons and psychobabble, to his thrashing legs pounding her calves black and blue while she tried to sleep.

The sex had been at least cathartic, like a good cry, and her back and shoulders felt relaxed, as if they had been massaged. She felt cleansed physically, but was also aware of a complete lack of connection. Elias wasn't a bad lover, just distant. There was an impersonal aspect to his lovemaking, and Denise was reminded of her dentist, who overbooked his schedule and always got her name wrong when she went in for a checkup. In bed, Elias was the same way, always seemingly distracted by something that had nothing to do with her. She supposed she was reminded of the dentist because both a dental exam and sex required close physical contact, and to have the other person not focus on her made her feel slightly dehumanized. It was yet another characteristic she could overlook because of his mother's death. She understood. If her own mother had been murdered, wouldn't she also have developed some of those characteristics?

She looked at Elias, who was seemingly uncomfortable even in sleep. Perhaps her protective feelings were triggered by the guilt she must be feeling for doing a background check on him, and finding out the fact in the first place. Then there was the guilt over the fact itself. Did the job have anything to do with it? Was her employment in the FBI – who had failed, like the LAPD, to solve the case – another source of internal guilt? Was she holding herself responsible for the failure to find Elias's mother's killer? Is that why she had gone to bed with him?

Oh God, who cared. Her skull was pounding and she needed coffee.

Elias sighed heavily and then rolled into his pillow, his face away from her, his body still. Denise gently lifted the covers, feeling the shock as the cool air rushed over her legs under the down comforter. She quickly dropped the comforter back down, the warmth settling over her legs again. That felt good. Her head hurt, but it was cold out in the world, and maybe it was best to lie there for a little while longer. She looked at Elias, breathing heavily, then his legs thrashed quickly, as if intentionally kicking her. She started, and checked his face to make sure he was actually asleep. He was.

Elias thrashed again and she'd had enough. She quickly lifted the covers and got out of the bed, shivering, stepping lightly and quickly as she looked around the room for her clothes. It always amazed her how her clothing could become so randomly distributed by sex. Everything she had worn was always scattered, even when the sex wasn't that passionate. She found her bra, panties and blouse, then noticed Elias was starting to stir, and she didn't want any face to face contact with him, not yet. Actually, never again would be fine, too, but she hadn't yet reached enough time and distance from the event to admit that to herself. So she quickly pulled on one of Elias's shirts and picked up his slippers and the rest of her clothes, and tiptoed towards the door.

Blood on the carpet. Denise noticed a white throw rug with bloodstains on it, not much blood, but enough to make her look twice. It reminded her of her training classes at Quantico, where they had described what blood looked like in each stage of drying, what each pattern indicated. She had loved that class. She had real energy and excitement about the FBI back then. This blood was days old. Almost wistfully, she leaned over to get a closer look, examining the pattern. It was a drip pattern. Someone with a slight wound had stood directly over the rug. Maybe Elias had been trying his hand at carpentry and paid the price. Carpentry? Elias? Probably not. Maybe he had cut himself on a pen cap. She shrugged and went downstairs to look for coffee.

The kitchen, like the rest of the house, had unrealized potential, but Denise decided that the need for redecoration here was most pronounced. You could get away with 1960s furniture in the living room or dining room, but appliances needed to be changed out. It was clear that Elias changed things out only when the last possible drop of earthly use had been rung out of them, resulting in a shiny, buffed steel dishwasher with an electronic control panel crammed next to a garbage disposal from the 1970s with stained and yellowed buttons. In the laundry room she saw the same picture, an ultramodern dryer next to a dismal and decrepit washing machine. Despite last night's moments of flamboyance with his hundred dollar bills, Elias, she decided, was not one to throw his money around.

She opened the first cupboard and found bottles of wine. They all had discount stickers on them from the same wine store. Denise rolled her eyes. She opened the next cupboard, where she found the coffee, also a discount brand. Shit. He didn't like to spend money on anything, and Denise liked high-end coffee. Sure enough, the filters she found were the recycled newspaper ones, a thousand for a dollar. She filled the coffee maker and looked for a spoon, where she found a wine tool with blood on it. So that was how he had cut himself. Definitely not carpentry.

While she was waiting for the coffee to brew, she

began to snoop around. Cautiously, in case anything like brooms and mopheads came spilling out, she opened the door to the pantry, and examined the stockpiles of canned food. Bored, she shut it and opened another door, this one to the basement. It was dark, but at the top of the steps she saw some shelves. There was just enough light to make out a pile of extension cords and a staple gun covered in rust. Next to them were four or five empty beer bottles. Bored again, she shut the door, picked a mug from the dish rack and poured herself a cup of coffee while the machine was still brewing.

She went out onto the back deck, which was small but comfortable, and where the decades-old metal porch furniture seemed to gracefully blend with the timeless view of the overgrown yard and the fifty-foot maples. She sat down in a wrought-iron chair and sipped her coffee, taking in the view, enjoying the total silence of a weekend morning here in the boonies. She hoped Elias would not wake up until after she had gone. It would be nice to have a little alone time in his house, getting the full benefit of such a beautiful environment, which she imagined he either took for granted or had never appreciated. He seemed the type to find nature an annoyance, to focus on the acorns falling on his car rather than appreciate the tree.

She doubted the alone time would happen, though. Unfortunately, men always seemed to feel some sense of obligation to wake up and make awkward conversation. But maybe he'd be a late sleeper. She'd leave a nice note on his kitchen table, and began composing it in her head. Dear Elias. Should she spell his name right or wrong? An intentional misspelling was a nice subtle touch that she didn't want to see him again. How could you misspell Elias? It was one of those names that spelt themselves. Any misspelling would make her look like an idiot.

How about just . . . Elias? No dear. No, way too impersonal. Denise didn't want to come off as bitchy. How about "Hey!" Sounded goofy. How about nothing, no note. Just take off?

She heard a rustling and suddenly realized there was a person no more than fifteen feet from her, a young woman on the other side of the fence.

"Hey, professor," the girl called playfully. She parted the shrubs around the fence and peered through and saw Denise, sitting in a metal chair in her underwear, wearing one of Elias's shirts. "Oh," she said, disappointed. The shrubs came back together, and the girl walked off.

This was too weird. Denise stood up, tossed the cheap, crappy coffee in the bushes, went inside, put on her skirt and blouse, quietly called a taxi on her cellphone, and left. She walked to the end of the street to wait for the cab. The note on the table said, "Bye".

* * *

Just from looking through the cracks in the blinds, Elias could tell it was going to be a beautiful day. Already the sun was gleaming in streaks across the room, illuminating dust particles floating absently through space on their way to join the billions of others on his dresser. The streaks of sunlight reminded him that he needed a cleaning woman. Perhaps he'd put up a note on the bulletin board in the student union. Hire some freshman cutie for ten dollars an hour to finally get this old, decaying wood dusted. How about eight dollars an hour? Would anyone do it for eight?

He caught a whiff of a woman's perfume and snapped fully awake, remembering the night before and noticing for the first time Denise's absence in the bed. He strained to hear the noise of the shower, or a clattering of cupboard doors in the kitchen, wondered if she was in the house, but it was stone quiet. The bitch had just left. Probably called a cab. He could smell coffee. He wondered if she had left any for him.

He had a slight feeling of post-sex euphoria, which evaporated the instant he remembered Dixon was there. It was Sunday, and now he would probably have to manufacture a reason to go into the college. Today was the first day since Dixon had arrived that Elias wanted the house to himself, and he resented the man not as an armed intruder but as a room-mate. Today would be a good day to get the paper, have coffee on the back deck, and get some writing done.

He still hadn't heard from any of the journals that had received his article. How long did it take? In the end he had decided to take Ann's advice and re-write certain paragraphs, just to make it clearer that he didn't agree with the National Socialist Party – he just understood how others could, given the era. Well, clearly a lot of them had, so wouldn't it be a good idea to publish an article that examined why? Wouldn't that make the world a better place, publishing an analysis of people getting caught up in war hysteria? He wished he could just walk around his house naked and write and daydream about getting published in the *Historical Review*, but he couldn't, because Dixon was here.

Elias got up, stretched, peed, and went downstairs in his undershorts. He opened the front door to let some air in, then went and opened the back door to get the air current running through the house. On his way through the kitchen, he noticed Denise's empty coffee mug, rinsed, in the sink. He stood on the back deck for a moment, feeling the warmth of the sunlight, wondering where he'd left his sunglasses, when he heard a floorboard creak behind him.

He spun around, startled, and saw Dixon not five feet

away, shirt off, eyes cold and distant. He was holding a pipe wrench.

Elias started instantly calculating how quickly he could get away from Dixon if the pipe wrench started to move up. He figured if he could get six or seven inches closer to the doorknob, he could slam the door while diving off the deck, giving him ample time to get up and run to the Covington house while Dixon was opening the door. But getting closer to the doorknob meant getting closer to Dixon. So it wasn't going to happen.

But if Dixon took another step, he'd be off running. And to hell with this whole situation, it wasn't worth it. He'd run down the street screaming that he'd fucked Melissa. He'd tell everyone. He'd tell Melissa's dad, that over-coiffed lawyer in his immaculate blue shirts who seemed incapable of parking entirely on his own property. He'd tell him right to his face, while his plastic-surgery victim of a wife wept openly through healing tear ducts. And then he'd give him the finger and move out of Tiburn for good. But he wasn't going to get beaten to death on his back porch by a maniac just because he was keeping secrets.

"There's no way to hit someone with one of these and just make it hurt," Dixon said.

Elias didn't move.

"Three or four pound piece a' cast iron," Dixon said,

tossing it like a horseshoe at Elias's bare feet, where it clanked onto the porch and made him dance to avoid it. Elias looked reproachfully at Dixon, who was clearly aware that it might well have broken some bones in his foot. Dixon just stared back, then pulled a pack of cigarettes out of his pocket, stepped past Elias onto the deck, and lit one.

"I realized that, when that woman opened the door to the basement. I was holding that pipe wrench, under the stairs, trying not to breathe," Dixon said, staring off thoughtfully into the trees. "I thought, if she comes down the stairs, I'll just knock her out. Then I'll tie her up and get the fuck outta here."

He exhaled a long drag, and sat down in one of the metal chairs. "But then I thought, that's really not what's gonna happen. I'm gonna swing this at her head, and there's gonna be that sound. Kind of like an egg breakin'. Know what I'm talking about?"

Elias shook his head.

"I saw it once. My first stint. There was this junkie, they'd just bought him in for, like, mugging or purse snatching or some shit. He knocked over some old lady, pushed her down some steps and fucked up her hip. Turned out she was the grandmother of one of the dudes doing a serious stretch. Three days later, in the machine shop, bam, right on his head with a hammer. Sounded like an egg breaking."

Elias nodded. Dixon had a way with a story, not weighing it down with detail. Where was this one heading? Not to a bashing, apparently, because Dixon had tossed the pipe wrench aside. Should he ask a question? Did Dixon want to talk?

"I was helping clean out the freezer in the morgue when his family came in, day or two later. You wouldn't a' thought a junkie had so many people cared about him, you know? There was this one girl, like eighteen maybe, I figured it was his sister. Beautiful. Tall girl, long legs, wearing a flowery blue dress like you'd wear to church. The minute she saw the junkie dude laid out on the slab, she just sobbed. Howled like a fuckin' coyote till they took her away."

Elias didn't like this story. He had gotten laid last night and it was a beautiful morning and he had come downstairs in a good mood. He needed to get out of here and get to his office and not listen to anymore.

"They had a viewing in the prison morgue?" he asked, trying to sound interested.

"If that woman had come down the stairs," Dixon said, ignoring him. " Bam."

There were a few beats of silence, enough time for an opening for a subject change. "Yeah. It might have been a little risky, now that I think about it. I won't do that again, though," He sighed. "Hey, I've gotta get to the office, got a lot of work to catch . . ."

222

"I would have killed her," Dixon said, looking right at Elias, his voice not raised at all to speak over him, almost as if he was talking to himself.

Elias stopped talking.

"It's not just your life you're fucking with."

"No, I understand that." Elias nodded sheepishly like a fourth-grader in the principal's office.

"The family came in for the personal effects. The effects room and the morgue were the same room. Just a coincidence," Dixon said, and Elias realized he had heard him earlier. The man seemed to keep two things going on in his mind at the same time, an indicator of intelligence which, in this case, Elias found frightening. Depending on the individual, a skill which was generally associated with good grades could also be used, Elias thought, to chat amiably about the weather while examining a throat for slitting. Or a head for bashing. "What if I'd snored?"

"What?"

"What if I was asleep when she came downstairs, and I'd been snoring? What then? What if she'd noticed you don't drink beer and took one of those beer bottles I leave at the top of the steps? Took it back to her lab and printed it? What then?"

"Why would she do that?"

"Pipe wrench is no good." Dixon was ignoring him again, listening to his own mind instead of Elias's questions. "I don't know how to use it. I want my gun back." Dixon drew hard on the cigarette, then flicked it into the yard.

Elias nodded. Oh shit. He couldn't give the gun back. He remembered how terrified he had been of Dixon when Dixon had the gun. He wasn't going back to that situation. He'd go to the cops. He should go to the cops today.

"The gun's at the office," Elias said evenly. Dixon nodded. Elias wondered if Dixon had looked around the house for it, snooped through his things. He had stashed the gun under the spare tire in his car.

"You understand why I want it back?" Dixon asked.

"Yeah," Elias said quickly, and he realized that his capitulation in this matter, in handing so much power back to him with so little argument, was making Dixon suspicious. "I mean, I'd rather keep it, but I understand."

Dixon was looking at him, and Elias felt he was being evaluated, and that Dixon was reading his mind. Dixon was understanding that there was no way Elias was going to give him the gun back. Dixon was completely aware Elias was just blowing smoke and trying to get away from him. Dixon was about to do something explosive.

But Dixon just nodded thoughtfully. "OK," he said. "You're going to go get me the gun . . . today?"

224

"Yes," said Elias, careful not to move a muscle unless the movement portrayed the picture of honesty he was trying to project.

Dixon shrugged. "All right then," he said. "I need a carton of cigarettes and a six pack of my beers, too. And my hundred-and-twenty cash." He slammed the door behind him when he went back in.

Elias exhaled, and felt himself starting to sweat. He felt like the whole day had been ruined. No post-sex euphoria anymore.

He needed Dixon gone.

11

Elias pulled out of the driveway, sure that Dixon was crouched low by the window and watching him leave. The guy had just let him go, and he really seemed to believe Elias was coming back. *Give you your gun back . . . Are you out of your fucking mind? Yeah, I'm going to get you your shopping list: beer, cigarettes, a newspaper, and something you can murder me with before you leave, you psychopath.*

He drove off, carefully suppressing the impulse to slam his foot on the gas and squeal out of there. The whole time he had been dressing in his bedroom his heart had been pounding, listening for the creak of Dixon's foot on the stairs. Dixon must know he was going to opt out of their arrangement. He was coming up the stairs, with the pipe wrench. He was going to throw open the door and his face would be maniacal and he would scream, "Trying to fuck me, eh?"

Bam.

He had wanted to pull on a T-shirt because, alone, in his room, his hands had been shaking so badly he couldn't button anything. But he had told Dixon he was going into the office, and even Dixon would think a professor going into work in a T-shirt with holes in it was funny. Even on a Sunday. Elias was always immaculately dressed when he went to work, Dixon must have noticed that. Then he had pulled his dress pants off the chair and noticed the foot-wide bloodstain, which had been concealed from Denise's view by the way they had been carelessly thrown onto the chair the night before. Lucky.

The buttoning process had taken so long that he had needed to steady his breathing, and when the shirt was finally on, he still had to deal with his shoes. In his haste, he had pulled on white socks. He couldn't wear white socks with black loafers, and he didn't want to take his socks off, because his hands were shaking again. So he pulled some sneakers out of the closet. Dress pants and sneakers. Would Dixon notice that this just wasn't something he did?

Hell, it was Sunday. And he needed to get out of the house.

When he had come galloping down the stairs, his instinct had been to keep up his speed when he came to the ground and flee the house. But through the open kitchen door he had noticed Dixon sitting on his metal deck chair, smoking. The guy had been outside, not seeming to care where Elias was. Maybe he hadn't been suspicious after all. Maybe I've really fooled him, Elias had thought. Nonetheless, he hadn't waited to double-check his briefcase. He had quickly grabbed it, and was just turning to leave when Dixon had stood up with a growl, and came into the kitchen.

Elias had tried not to act like he was about to run, had just kept moving smoothly towards the door.

"Get me a Sunday paper," Dixon had called after him jauntily. "I really should be keeping up with the world."

Now, out of the house at last, he began to plan his next move. He needed to calm down. Find a coffee shop somewhere in which he could organize his thoughts. But as he felt himself decompressing, his mind began to wander back to the sex of the night before. Elias had felt so much pleasure in having her so close to solving her crime, it had actually made the sex better. He had been fantasizing at the moment of orgasm, wondering if screaming out some kind of muffled clue would be his ultimate inside joke. "Basement!" His mind had become cloudy with pleasure and he had gotten lost in the moment, but afterwards, he must have been grinning, because Denise had commented on it.

"You sure look happy after sex," she had said. For her part, she had seemed vague and distant. Most likely having those deep after-sex thoughts that Elias would rather not hear. He had fallen asleep quickly.

He drove slowly past the town square, and was pleased to see that Willard's Coffee Shop was open. He parked, got a twenty-ounce cappuccino, found a seat at a table on the deck. And he sat there, sipping cappuccino, thinking about going to the police department, which was fifty feet away.

Denise pulled out onto the highway, glad to be rid of Kohl on the drive back, to be able to pick her own radio station and not worry about making conversation. She could stop for coffee or a burger wherever she wanted. Lately she wondered if she enjoyed being alone far too much.

Goodbye to Tiburn, she thought as she accelerated up the on-ramp and joined the sparse traffic on I-93 South. It was a pretty place, but she was never going back there. It had left her with a feeling that was not quite right. Something had happened to her the minute she had arrived there, a complete loss of self, which one usually associated with places like Bangkok or Las Vegas. A new Denise had emerged, a pot-smoking, promiscuous Denise, who needed to go back in her cage now that she was on the way back to New York City.

She had no feelings of guilt. She was far too lapsed a Catholic for that. What she had was a vague sense that something bad had happened to her spiritually, a mild, nagging feeling of indefinable violation, as if her apartment had been broken into but everything left untouched. She tried to overcome the feeling by focusing on the mundane matters of her return home. Dry cleaning. How late were the dry cleaners open on Sunday? Till five? She looked at the dash panel clock. 9:02. She had eight hours to return the rental car on Tenth Avenue and get to Wang's Dry Cleaners, or she wasn't going to have anything to wear tomorrow. Maybe she should just call out. Nope, couldn't do that, Carver would expect a report before lunch.

The feeling didn't go away.

Her cellphone, which she had laid out on the passenger seat, rang once, and she answered without taking her eyes off the road to see who it was. Calls on a Sunday morning were usually friendly in nature and never required a professional greeting, so she just said, "Hello?"

"Is this . . . Denise?"

"Yes." She recognized Elias's voice immediately. Oh, shit. Should have just let it ring. Be businesslike, end the conversation quickly. Pretend you don't know who it is. "Who's this?"

There was a silence, and she thought something might not be right with Elias. But then, she had always had that feeling with him.

"Elias White," Elias said. "How are you?"

"I'm good," said Denise. "I'm about to stop for coffee. I'm on the highway." She had just passed a sign that said "Next exit eighteen miles".

"You never said goodbye," Elias said, and she didn't think he sounded hurt, just curious. Would this be a good time to just hang up and pretend her cellphone had died? Maybe she should start making hissing noises like she was entering a dead area, then shut the phone off. No, he'd just call back later, when other people were around.

"You were dead asleep," Denise said.

"Yeah," said Elias, and there was a silence again, leaving Denise wondering if he just wanted to chat. If that was the case, she had to end it now. He hadn't seemed the type to get emotional over a one-night stand. Denise had figured Elias as being an old hand at them, which was why she had chosen him.

"Well," said Denise, with as much finality as she could muster. "Thanks for everything. I had a nice time."

"Listen," Elias said quickly, as if he had sensed her desire to end the conversation, and was trying to keep it going. "I wanted to ask you something."

"Uh huh."

There was a second or two of silence. He had slowed down again now he knew she was listening. "I wanted to ask you about the bank robber. How's the investigation going?"

"I can't discuss an ongoing investigation," she said. Had he really called for that? Denise now had the sense that maybe he was upset she had just left, was looking for some kind of connection. She thought there had been an understanding of meaninglessness.

"Oh."

"Well, OK then." She actually tapped the brake pedal as if she was moving onto an exit ramp, hoping that Elias might notice the noise of deceleration and believe her story of pulling off to get coffee. As she crested a hill, she took in the view of the New Hampshire mountains, forests lining both sides of the road, and she realized she couldn't see a car in either direction. Nothing but empty highway, mountains and trees. A view she could be enjoying if she could only hang up. "I'm going to get some coffee. Thanks again."

"I'm across the street from the police station," said Elias.

That was weird. Why was he telling her that? "What are you doing at the police station?"

"I'm not at the police station. I'm across the street. At a coffee shop."

"Yeah," said Denise. "Coffee sounds about right. I'm pulling up to a rest stop myself." She pulled the car over onto the shoulder and came to a complete stop, and hoped he heard the unmistakable sound as she yanked up the parking brake. It might be time to break out the hissing sounds. "Okey doke," she said. "I'll talk to you later."

"Uh huh. Bye," Elias said, and she almost thought she heard dejection in his voice, but she slammed the cellphone shut before she could get a chance to analyze it. She tossed the phone back on the seat as if it were red hot, relieved to have it out of her hands. It bounced off the passenger seat, rebounded off the glove compartment, and landed on the floor mat.

The vague sense of violation had gotten worse. It must have something to do with Elias. Maybe it *was* some deep-seated Catholic guilt about the one-night stand. She'd had them before, in New York, and not felt this way. Maybe she was just getting too old for them. She put the cellphone back on the seat, then opened the glove box to look at her rental contract, hoping to distract herself by focusing on details again. Where was the car rental return? Tenth Avenue and what?

She looked over the document, trying to find the address, and there was too much small print. Irritated, she shoved the papers back into the glove box and slammed it shut, and as she pulled back onto the deserted road, she was overwhelmed by the feeling that she needed to take a shower. She felt filthy. She had showered barely an hour ago at the Tiburn motel.

She gunned the car up to highway speed and realized she couldn't wait to get back to New York City, to the life she had been so anxious to get a break from only two days before. She wanted that easy anonymity, that feeling that any story of hers could be topped by the next person rounding the corner. But it wasn't really so much the city she needed. She just needed to get as far away as possible from Tiburn, and never go back.

Elias put his cellphone back on the table and looked at it, his hands over his mouth as if trying to stop secrets from coming out. He had almost told Denise everything.

For half an hour he had sat there, staring into his cappuccino froth, readying himself for the walk over to the police station. How would he phrase it? "There's a bank robber hiding in my house." And he'd wait for the response. Would they frantically reach for phones with urgent looks on their faces the minute he began to speak? Or would they stare at him blankly? Then, during the course of the half hour, Elias had noticed that no one had come or gone from the police building, and the lobby, which he could see through the glass door, was dark.

The police building shared space with the municipal building, and it was closed on Sundays. The police station was closed. That was great. Elias was thinking about handing the local cops what was probably the biggest case in their history, but it would have to wait until Monday.

It gave him a few extra minutes to think. He imagined them surrounding his house, calling to Dixon through megaphones. They would probably call a SWAT team down from Concord, line the street with dark blue vans which would spill out men in black body armor, sniper rifles and baseball caps. Melissa and her family would be out in the street, looking bemused, along with Mr Cuthbertson, who would probably be wearing gloves and holding pruning shears as the helmeted men with M-16s ordered them to go back into their houses.

Dixon, of course, would not come out, and they would fire tear gas into the house. Tear gas. Elias hadn't thought of that. That stuff would get into his carpet, his couch pillows, his bedspread. And the actual canister would be fired through a glass window. Who was going to pay for the damage? The bank whose money Elias was going to help them recover? Doubtful. And what if shooting started? Did he really want M-16 bullets going through Dixon's head and into the new Sony DVD player, splattering brain matter across his Nakamichi speakers?

And that was the best case scenario. Elias couldn't be sure Dixon would opt to go out in a blaze of glory. Maybe he'd come right out, give himself up, let himself be cuffed right in front of Mr Cuthbertson, Melissa, and her odd family. And as they dragged him away, he'd give Elias the eye as he was shoved into the back of a van by six helmeted men with rifles, a look that said, that's it, I'm telling them everything.

Then it would be evening, and he would be sitting on his metal porch chair, the street quiet now, except for colleagues and neighbors calling and asking if he was OK. And then, after the furor had died down, maybe three days later, he would be sitting at his desk in his office and Alice would knock gently and say, with that disturbed expression of hers, that the police were here. Something about Elias's teenage neighbor . . .

So maybe going to the police wasn't such a great idea. Then he thought about Dixon in his basement, with the gun. What was worse, getting a visit from the cops, or being found by them after his body had started to smell up the neighborhood?

That was when he had thought about Denise and started fantasizing about her fixing everything.

He could call her. He could tell her she had just spent the night in a house with the felon she was looking for. She might actually be able to solve this problem. Maybe he could arrange it so that Denise would go downstairs with her gun drawn and just shoot Dixon five or six times before the guy had a chance to open his mouth. He could tell her about what a monster Dixon was, how Dixon had terrified Elias into some kind of shock.

But then, when he had actually called her and heard her voice, it suddenly seemed insane to tell her. He had pulled it off, made a complete fool out of her, and now he was going to call her and confess? Her voice was so cold and distant, so anxious to be rid of him, that he had stalled, enjoying her ignorance. He wanted her to know how badly he had fooled her – only not badly enough to go on trial for statutory rape of a minor.

And so he had put the cellphone down, covered his mouth, breathed deeply and taken another sip of his cappuccino. Through the picture window of the coffee shop, he could see a phone book sitting on the counter of the cash register. He went inside and asked to borrow it, then took it back to the table and flipped back through the yellow pages.

Gift shops, graphic design, guest houses. Guns and gunsmiths.

Putting the phone book in his lap, he carefully tore the page out, shifting in his chair to cover the noise of the paper ripping. He folded the page under the table and put it in his pocket, then returned the book to the register.

Dixon leaned back in the deck chair, shut his eyes, felt the sun in his face, and listened to the sound of peace in Elias's backyard. Today was Sunday. He would stay with this fuck-up one more day and then be on his way. Monday was always a bad day to travel, too much business. Tuesdays were better. You could get lost in the anonymity of the working week. Good day to take the train.

The bushes parted and Dixon's heart jumped, and before he could move and dart back into the house, he found himself looking at a pretty teenage girl holding a kitten. The same girl who had been looking for her bra on Elias's living room floor just a week before.

"Hi," she said, petting the kitten, not seeming surprised to see Dixon. She was looking around, behind him, into the house, and Dixon figured right away she was trying to get a handle on the situation. Dixon had heard her surprise the FBI lady earlier in the morning, and now she had returned for more information, using the kitten as an innocent prop.

Holding the bewildered kitten in an outstretched hand, she put one leg over the fence, shifted the kitten from one hand to the other, then put the other leg over, to come uninvited into Elias's yard.

"This is Tyke," she said, holding the kitten out for Dixon's examination. Wordlessly, and while still trying to figure how to handle this, Dixon instinctively reached for the kitten, and she handed it to him. It mewed as the girl deposited it into his huge hand.

"I'm Melissa," she said. "Who're you?"

He was stumped. How to answer that? Should have thought of a fake name. "Phil . . . Johnson," finally came out, rough, gravelly, unsure. Just what he didn't want. But the girl was barely listening, seemed more concerned with stealing glances back into the kitchen, as if wondering where Elias was.

"Elias had to go to work today," Dixon offered.

"Mm hmm," she said, as if she didn't care. "Are you a friend of his?"

"Yeah." Dixon gently petted the kitten, which was moving nervously around in his hand, looking up at him, trembling. He knew his answers weren't satisfying the girl's curiosity, and the last thing he wanted was for her to leave while wanting to know more. He needed to make up a good story. "Me and my girlfriend are staying with him for the weekend," he said.

"Ah, so that was your girlfriend . . . that lady I saw this morning?"

"Yeah. You saw her?" Dixon was almost tempted to ask what she looked like. "She had to leave early, go back to Jersey. She's gotta work tomorrow."

"Yeah. She looked upset," said Melissa. She sat on the steps. Sitting down wasn't good, because it meant she wasn't leaving soon. Dixon couldn't help but admire her long, muscular legs, suddenly aware that he hadn't seen a woman up close in days, if not weeks. He petted the kitten, which kept moving around in his hand, and he held it to his chest.

"How old is this little guy?" Dixon asked, hoping to deflect the conversation to a more neutral topic.

"Six weeks," she said. "His mom had a litter of four." She looked at him, her eyes bright, her voice full of youthful enthusiasm. "You want him?"

Dixon laughed at the idea. "Nahh."

240

"Why not? He likes you."

Dixon paused. Why not? Maybe he'd need a little bit of companionship, and the kitten would be just the thing. But he couldn't bother with anything like that until he got across the Canadian border. He was sure they had kittens in Canada. It would have to wait.

"I'm gonna be on the road some, over the next month or so. This little dude here wouldn't like it." He handed her the kitten back, and it tried to dig its claws into his hand to prevent the transfer. It really did seem to like him, and he felt a sudden rush of sadness that he had to let it go, that he was always having to let everything go, so he could run to somewhere else. This sadness was accompanied by a feeling of anticipation, of the relief he would feel when he finally bought his farm. A home, a real home for the first time. He could have a kitten if he felt like it, or a puppy, or chickens and cows, or alpacas that would spit on him and bite him. And as Melissa took the kitten back, he felt better, because he had been worrying about details when she came across the fence, and now he realized it was going to be all right. Everything was going to be all right, and soon this pile of shit that had been his life in the United States was going to be over.

Melissa laughed as she held the kitten up playfully. "On the road some," she mimicked him. "Where are you from?"

"Kentucky," he said, standing up, an invitation to end the conversation politely, and Melissa stood up too, sensing the dismissal. He liked that about her, that she understood. She seemed like a nice girl. Very pretty, a little ditzy, young, but OK. "I'll tell Elias you stopped by."

"OK," she said, hopping off the steps. She went back as if to climb over the fence again, and Dixon suggested she just go through the gate and around the house.

"I don't mind," she said brightly, and exited the way she had come.

Dixon felt so much better from chatting with a stranger that it didn't bother him for a few moments that someone other than Elias had seen him in Tiburn. It didn't matter anymore. All this would be over soon.

Elias pulled up outside Wicker Guns 'n Ammo, and with the car still idling in the empty parking lot, stared into the dusty darkness of the store. He knew it was open on Sunday because he had called from a payphone. He hadn't wanted his cell number on the store's caller ID, in case something went wrong and he had to run out. He didn't know what could possibly go wrong, but he just had a vague feeling something might.

Elias popped the trunk of his car and pulled Dixon's shiny pistol from underneath the oily clutter of metal objects fastened below his spare tire. He looked at it for the first time, felt its considerable weight. There was power in the weight, and he found that he liked holding it.

He walked into the gun shop, and a bell over the door jangled. This was one of those country businesses Elias had grown to despise, because the proprietors always had a sense of localism, self-righteousness born of a tangible feeling of superiority to outsiders. Outsiders included any member of the general public who had never visited the establishment before, and Elias always marveled that they could stay in business.

As he entered, he held the pistol tightly in his hand, and wondered if this made for a more impressive entrance. He wanted to appear confident and familiar with the firearm. Just a guy buying bullets for some range shooting. He saw the shopkeeper behind the counter, and he wondered if walking into the store with the pistol in his hand looked like a stick-up. He loosened his grip on the gun and made sure he smiled and nodded when he met the man's eye.

The gun-shop owner was in his fifties, a kindly-looking, bespectacled man, and Elias imagined he had a son or daughter who attended Tiburn, probably on some kind of scholarship. He doubted this gun store covered the expense of on-campus living, so he figured the child drove the half hour every day, maybe even worked in the store part-time. He noticed a wedding ring and tried to picture the man's wife, figured she was friendly and open but very unsure of people not from around here.

"Hi," said Elias. "I got a problem with this here." This here. Try to talk like a local. Relax, you *are* a local. He laid the gun down on the counter and the man, who had given a perfunctory nod, less friendly than Elias had hoped for, looked at the gun quickly.

"Nice piece," he said. "You don't see too many of these around anymore." The man picked it up and turned it over. "What's the problem? You want a magazine?"

"A magazine? Oh, no, I need bullets." Suddenly nervous about having his pretence of knowledge and experience with the pistol exposed, he picked up a box of bullets sitting in a nearby display and examined it. "I think these were the ones I had last time."

The man wordlessly took the box of bullets from his hand and placed them back in the display pile, then tilted his glasses off his nose and turned the pistol over in his hand.

"The serial number's filed off," he said.

Elias said nothing, feeling panic rising. His impulse was to grab the gun back and run out the door, but he just stood there, frozen, waiting. In that panicked second, he imagined the store owner reading his license plate as he peeled off into the parking lot, or the man ripping a shotgun off the wall and blasting him in the back as he bolted for the door. So he waited, frozen, for the man to reach for the phone to call the cops, or pull a pistol of his own, this one loaded, from behind the counter.

"You don't want those bullets, not with an M1911," the man said finally. "Those're hollow points. They'll jam it." He put the pistol back down on the counter and turned around, muttering to himself, looking at rows and rows of bullet boxes. "Oh, no. You want a full metal jacket." Elias felt a wave of relief wash over him as he realized the man was not going to pursue the question of why the serial number was filed off. The shopkeeper selected one box, extracted it, examined the print on the side, then plopped them on the counter.

"These're what you're looking for," he said. "It's a 230-grain. Forty-five cal. Remember that for next time." He walked to the ancient cash register, paused, then rang the order up. "Eighteen dollars," he said.

Elias quickly extracted a twenty from his wallet, noticing that it was one of the four twenties he was supposed to have given Dixon. The man gave him two dollars change while Elias examined his purchase and noticed that the price wasn't on the bullets. Was he being overcharged, because his ignorance was obvious? Because the man knew he was buying bullets for a pistol with the serial number filed off?

"Pricey," Elias observed, hoping the man would infer from this that he bought bullets all the time. He instantly regretted the comment, even though it drew no response. To repair the relationship he felt he had just damaged, he said, "I was shooting just last week, and I was thinking of selling it. What kind of money could I get for it?"

The man tilted his glasses, looked at it again. "This gun hasn't been fired in months," he said. "And no one's going to buy it with the number filed down. If I were you, I'd get rid of it."

The man didn't turn or leave after he was done talking, but he was clearly expecting Elias to do so. He was looking at the ground.

"What . . . what . . ." Elias felt curiously compelled to ask questions about the gun, to somehow engage this man in a conversation, to make him understand that he was an intelligent and worthwhile human being who just wanted to buy bullets. "What . . . er, is this model called? An M1119, did you call it?"

The man turned to him quizzically and shook his head, and Elias felt he was at last being acknowledged. "It's an M1911-A1," he said, and Elias noticed the kindly father with a child who went to Tiburn again, for an instant. "It was designed in 1911, and . . ."

"It's that old?" Elias realized he sounded like one of his students, who didn't really care about the subject but was trying to get his professor to notice him.

"It was *designed* in 1911," the man went on with the exaggerated patience of someone becoming gradually more irritated. "This is a later model. And if I were you, I'd get rid of it."

"Yes, you're probably right," said Elias. "I just wanted to fire it first." Aware that he was now admitting that he hadn't just fired it last week, he was overwhelmed again by the desire to run from the gun shop. But the admission seemed to make the shopkeeper warm to him, if only slightly.

"Do you need a magazine?" the shopkeeper asked.

Why did this man keep wanting to sell him magazines? "What kind of magazine? Like, you mean, a gun magazine?"

"Yes, a gun magazine. To load the bullets into."

Elias had read hundreds of history books, or at least flipped through them, and knew that a magazine was an important part of a firearm. But until that second, that piece of information hadn't processed in his mind, and he had assumed he was about to be handed reading material. He tried to make his sudden under-standing of the conversation unnoticeable by nodding thoughtfully.

"Yes. Yes," he said, nodding. "I'll take one of those, uh magazines. I do need that, too. I forgot."

"Without it you'd just be shoving the bullets into the grip," said the man, smiling for the first time.

Elias was so relieved to see a smile that he felt com-pelled to offer more information as fast as he could make it up, as if to cement a friendship that was forming between them. Between the guy who said bizarre untrue things about his pistol, and this intractable old bastard of a gun-shop owner.

"It was my father's gun," he said. "He just passed away. I just found it in the house. My father was a soldier in World War Two."

"This gun isn't military issue," said the shopkeeper, shaking his head, as if bored with Elias's lies. "This is chrome-plated. And it was manufactured well after that. If the serial number hadn't been filed off, I could tell you exactly when, but I figure, oh, about 1950s." He was looking at Elias now, as if he expected either honesty or silence. He slid a piece of black metal across the counter, then opened the box of bullets. "The war was over by then. You should learn about history," he said.

Elias was so taken aback by this country bumpkin telling him to learn about history that he almost blurted out that he was a history professor who was about to get tenure and was going to be published in the *National Historical Review*. Then he remembered, from deceiving Denise, the joy and energy that came from playing dumb. "My dad must have bought it recently, I guess," he said humbly.

The shopkeeper loaded bullets into the magazine. "This is how you load it," he said, pressing each bullet down into the clip with a slow, deliberate gesture, looking up at Elias to make sure he was being heeded. "It takes seven slugs." He slid the magazine into the grip. "This lever here drops the magazine back out of the grip when it's empty."

Elias nodded.

"Can you shoot, or do you need lessons?"

Elias clenched his lips, considering this. He couldn't shoot, but how hard was it? You pulled a trigger. But he might need a practice shot or two, to make sure the gun worked, to learn what it felt like. All kinds of disasters could happen without some experience with actually firing it, and this was clearly the man to ask for information.

"I charge twenty dollars for a fifteen-minute lesson," the shopkeeper said.

Now Elias felt he was being screwed again. This man was looking to take advantage of the poor sap who walked into his store just wanting to buy bullets. That was how these country types operated, Elias figured.

"I should be fine," he said. "Thanks, though."

"Fifteen even for the clip," said the shopkeeper, and Elias reached into his wallet again, making a mental note to research how much these things actually cost. He'd look it up online, see what they were selling for on eBay. As the man took his money and brought him change, Elias had the feeling that the shopkeeper knew exactly what he was going to do with the gun, and didn't really care. He must see people like me every day, Elias thought, people with sawn-off shotguns and filed-off serial numbers, people who lie about where they found the gun and what they were going to do with it.

"And five dollars change," the man said as he handed Elias a bill, slamming shut the register drawer.

"Thanks very much," Elias said, searching for eye contact, but the man had turned away again, walking to the back of the store, as if to escape Elias's company. "If I were you, I'd get rid of that thing," he said.

"Yes, of course. Thank you."

12

Elias was in a clearing, about three miles from Tiburn, looking at an overturned picnic table in what had been a small campground, known only to the locals. Now it was a field of ash and blackness, which – as he knew from an article last fall in the Tiburn *Register* – was because some high school kids had started a small forest fire. The fire had apparently been an accident, and they all had received community service, but Elias was surprised to see so much damage this long after the incident.

His mother had taken him here twice a month or so, and sometimes they would see deer. He was small enough then that deer were a cause for excitement. As an adult, he would come to dread them as nothing more than the leading local cause of car accidents, but back then, every deer was Bambi. The deer would never eat out of his hand, but he and his mother would wait, hopeful that one day it would happen, if only they could find the right food. They would sit and wait after having placed the food in a crude trail to the picnic table, listening for the sounds that indicated the deer's approach. Sometimes, they would wait for an hour or more, chatting about their days. Sometimes she would tell him stories.

It occurred to Elias, as he looked at the charred, overturned picnic table, that his mother had never expected the deer to approach them. As an adult, she must have known how timid they were, how impossible it was to win them over. The point of the exercise, for her, must have been the wait itself, and the conversations they would have. She had enjoyed his company then, when he was a little boy.

He had been standing here for at least five minutes, and there was no indication of human presence, which was just what he had been looking for. It was as quiet now as it had been when he had come here as a child. Still, you couldn't be too careful. He looked around, then around again, then acted as if he were going for a walk up a small path to the creek. A few steps up the path he finally became convinced the place was deserted, and he went back to his car.

He was surprised at how calm he felt. This wasn't as hard as he had always imagined it would be. He loosened the spare tire and pulled out Dixon's big, silver gun.

He walked out into the clearing again, looked around one final time. The pistol was heavy, but its weight was comforting, powerful. Quickly, Elias raised his arm, pointed the pistol at the picnic table and fired.

He felt the gun jump, as if it were a live cat trying to

escape his hand. The noise was deafening, yet somehow not unpleasant. He aimed at the table again, this time holding the pistol with both hands, one cupped underneath the grip. He fired again, and this time he had more control. Used to the noise now, but realizing it could be attracting attention from miles away, he fired a third time, then walked up to the picnic table. He saw three holes in the thick wood, not more than a foot apart.

He was a natural.

He got back in the car and drove back to Tiburn.

At the end of his street, Elias parked, the car idling, and took a deep breath. His hands were shaking, like they had been before he had taught his first class. He likened that experience to this one, remembering how the nervousness had made him perform better. Any undertaking which initiated change would inspire nervousness.

He reached down under the passenger seat and pulled the gun out from where he had stashed it. If he had been pulled over for some traffic offence, it wouldn't have been good to have the pistol sitting in plain view, with its serial number filed off. He looked at it, and felt a bolt of adrenaline go through him, tried to exhale the nervousness as if it were poisoned gas. Then he heard a low rumble coming up the street behind him, and in his wing mirror, he saw a kid on a skateboard, coming towards him.

Can't sit here all day, he thought to himself. He put the car in drive. Let's get this done. He saw the dashboard clock. 6:17.

He drove onto his street and into the driveway so fast that he had to slam on his brakes, and the gun slid off the passenger seat and onto the floor. He clenched his eyes shut in horror at what he had just done. What if the gun had gone off, shot him? Focused on the gun lying on the passenger-side floor, he leaned over to pick it up, and forgot the car was still in drive, and felt it creeping forward into his own hedges.

He gasped in exasperation, slammed the car into park. He was thinking too much. This was simple. He angrily picked the gun up off the floor of the car, checked to make sure the safety was off, and tucked it under his left arm as he got out and slammed the car door shut. Looking around, he noticed that the Covington house was quiet, and no cars were in the driveway. Good. They usually went out to dinner on Sunday afternoons. Keeping the pistol tucked in his armpit, he marched up onto his porch, flung his front door open, and looked around.

No one here.

There was a rustling from down in the basement as he heard Dixon get off his cot. He took the gun out from under his armpit. He opened the basement door and looked down, standing slightly to one side, the pistol concealed from the doorway.

Dixon hit the first of eight steps.

"Where you been, pardner?" Dixon was looking down as he climbed the stairs. Strangely, he seemed to be holding his side, the wound which hadn't seemed to hurt him in a week. He hit the second step. Elias could see him almost clearly now, in the light from the doorway.

Third step. Dixon was looking up at him now, seemed to notice something in Elias's expression, which changed his own, to confusion.

Elias moved in front of the doorway, and now the pistol was visible to Dixon. He moved his arm up so the gun was pointing straight into Dixon's chest.

The plan had been to fire the moment that motion had been completed, but he didn't. It was as if there was a small, forgotten part of Elias's brain that wanted to give Dixon another chance. He stood there, the pistol pointed at Dixon, who had frozen on the third step, staring at him. The look of confusion was gone, and Dixon's face was now impassive.

They stared at each other for a full two seconds.

"Fuck you," said Dixon. He sounded tired.

Elias pulled the trigger and was immediately surprised by the violence of Dixon's fall backward, as if he was being jerked back by a giant rubber band. Dixon had disappeared back into the darkness of the basement, and Elias heard some paint cans, which had been in a pyramid three high at the bottom of the stairs, crashing down. He heard Dixon make a noise, almost like a cow mooing, then sigh heavily. A hubcap fell off one of the shelves and began to spiral on the spot, making a noise that reached a crescendo, then was still.

Elias stood at the top of the stairs, his pistol still pointing at where Dixon had been, suddenly aware of the smoke, the smell of gunpowder. As if waking up, he fumbled for the light switch, and with the basement now illuminated, from his vantage point, he could see Dixon's feet. One of them was propped awkwardly over a paint can with brown paint dripped all over the side. The word "Whittaker Paints" was still readable.

Dixon's foot didn't move.

Elias didn't want to go downstairs and look. He stayed at the top of the stairs for a few seconds, and then sat down, his feet on the second step and his arm still extended, the pistol still pointing at Dixon's foot. He could hear himself breathing, became aware of how quiet the house was.

In the street, he heard the low rumble of the kid skateboarding, growing louder as it approached the house, then fading away again. It amazed him that the sounds out in the street were so familiar, while he was sitting at the top of his basement stairs in the middle of such an unfamiliar experience.

He looked at the clock on the kitchen wall. 6:20.

He stared for a few seconds at the smoke coming out of the pistol barrel, and felt a wave of relief. It was over. His house was his again. He could get on with his life.

He went down the stairs, and finally looked at Dixon, careful to have the pistol ready. He had seen so many horror movies where, at the end, the monster wasn't dead. He looked at Dixon's face, and Elias could recognize death right away. The eyes were half open, the muscles slack, the pose so unnatural. Nobody could fake like that.

Over on Dixon's cot, he saw the laundry bag full of money. He exhaled. What had Dixon said? People like money. That would help with the bills.

There was a science to this, Elias realized, a science that Dixon had probably been well aware of, but which was occurring to Elias only now. A hole in the backyard needed to be dug, and light was fading. The body had to be removed right away, and you couldn't do gardening at night. The Covingtons would look over the fence and notice. So it had to be done quickly.

Elias grabbed a rusted shovel that hadn't seen action since his mother had lived here, examined it, and was pleased to notice that it was of good quality. He rushed out into the yard and began to dig by the four dogwood trees which lined his property. It was the point of best concealment anywhere in his yard, and the logical place for such an undertaking. But the dogwoods had laid down some fierce roots, and he could barely get the shovel an inch into the earth. He started stabbing at the ground, trying to cut the roots with the shovel, and only when the shovel bounced back and injected two long splinters into his hand did he calm down and realize he was acting frantic.

Elias forced himself to walk, rather than run, into the house, then walked upstairs and began to change his clothes. In the back of his closet, he found an old T-shirt, some worn-out sneakers, and a pair of gym shorts he had used when painting the kitchen two years ago. They were crusty with white semi-gloss paint chips. Dressed in completely discardable clothing, he walked back downstairs, now humming to himself. He closed the kitchen door to the basement, then opened up the rusted metal doors at the top of a set of four concrete steps that led directly to the backyard. They creaked and groaned as he pushed them upward, and rust chips fell into his hair and got into his eyes. He shook them out and dusted himself off, propping the heavy doors open with the metal bars latched on the inside.

Perfect. Now he wouldn't have to carry Dixon up through the kitchen.

Then he removed the splinters from his hand with tweezers from the kitchen, and washed the blood away. He opened a bottle of wine, grabbed his cellphone, and went back to the yard. *Now* he looked like a guy who was doing some late evening Sunday gardening.

He found a new space, completely out in the open, and jammed the spade in. There was resistance in the first few inches, but as he dug down, the ground became soft and pliable. It had rained a lot lately, he figured, making the digging easier. He worked hard and steadily. After two hours, he was working in complete darkness, but he climbed out and looked at his handiwork with a sense of satisfaction he had never known from teaching. He had dug a grave.

Covered in earth, and with the bottle empty, he went back inside to open another. He swigged from it, went back outside and placed the new bottle beside the first, enjoying the visual image of the proof of inebriation in the scattered dirt. If someone happened upon the scene, God forbid, they would just think of him as a drunk eccentric. If only he had thought ahead and bought some hyacinths or a rhododendron bush from Billick's, he could actually do some late night planting and have a solid reason to explain this away. Next time this happens, he thought, I'll definitely buy some plants first. He giggled aloud at his own wit. Next time.

Back in the basement, he found some sturdy ropes, and fashioned a crude hoist which he pulled around Dixon's shoulders, going underneath each armpit. When he pulled Dixon's body towards the steps, amazed at how heavy he was, he realized that Dixon's head was flopping down at an awkward angle and would trap itself under each step. Aggravated, he cut another piece of rope and tied it in between the armpit struts, forming a workable cradle. He tried again to pull Dixon outside.

God, this guy was heavy. Were all bodies this hard to move? No wonder serial killers always hacked them up. Every few feet he had to stop and rest. He also had to keep stopping to push old lawnmowers and musty boxes of unread books out the way. The rope was cutting into his hands, and he had to stop to find a pair of gloves. Then he tripped on an unused bottle of motor oil and fell backwards onto the steps.

Elias picked himself up, scraped and cursing, and kicked the bottle of motor oil. Then, standing at the base of the cement steps, scraped and bleeding, he had an idea. He picked up the quart container of motor oil and dumped it all over the floor and steps, and, holding the rope outside, he yanked Dixon up out into his backyard. With the oil lubricating the process, Dixon slid across the floor and up the steps with ease. He'd remember that for next time, too. He giggled again.

His pride over this innovation gave him the energy to drag the body across the grass. As he arrived at the grave, panting, he heard his cellphone ringing. Still holding the rope in one hand, he answered it, trying not to sound out of breath.

"Elias White?" It was a man's voice. He hadn't recognized the number on his caller ID.

"Yes. This is Elias."

"Elias . . . this is Jim Skifford. I'm on the selection committee for the *Harvard Review*. We met at your college last year."

Elias knew the name immediately. Skifford had got his article. Excellent. Elias cradled the phone and dragged Dixon's body up to the grave. "Hi, Jim. Of course I remember you. I sent you an article recently."

"Yes," Skifford said, and Elias knew right away there was a problem. "Yes, I got it. I read it."

There was a pause. Elias wanted to wait until Skifford started talking again, but he couldn't contain himself. "And?" he asked anxiously. He lined Dixon's feet up with the grave. Perfect. It was long enough by over a foot.

"And, well, Professor, we've decided not to publish it."

Elias felt the deflation. He stood up straight, felt the tightness in his back from the rare bout of manual labor. "Why not?" he asked, trying to sound professional rather than wounded.

"Well, the . . . the diaries are, in some parts, interesting . . ."

Elias rubbed his dirt-covered hand across his brow. He leaned over again and rolled Dixon into the grave, where he landed with a thunk. "But?" he asked impatiently.

"But, Professor White, you can't honestly think we'd publish this."

"Why not?"

Jim Skifford sounded annoyed at having to explain himself further. "Because you seem to side with the people who wrote the diaries. I mean, for Pete's sake," he said, "there's a piece here from a German housewife who expresses joy that all the Jews in her neighborhood have disappeared."

"That's real," said Elias, grabbing the shovel. "That's history. She really wrote that." He pitched the first shovelful of dirt onto Dixon's body.

"Yes, but it's hardly illuminating," said Skifford. Then he asked, "Professor, are you busy now? Should we talk another time?"

"No, why?"

"You sound out of breath."

"Oh, no. I'm just working in my garden."

There was a pause, which Elias could only see as awkward.

"Ah, well," said Skifford. "Anyway, I just called to tell you the article has been rejected."

Elias didn't know what to say. Thank him for the consideration of a phone call? "Well, do you think it could be . . . worked on? And re-submitted?"

Skifford cleared his throat. "Not to us," he said.

"I just wanted to present a different point of view," Elias said, lamely, hoping to keep the conversation going, to elicit a word of encouragement or praise from this man. Nice effort, but no thanks, or excellent work, but we can't risk it. Skifford just sounded like he had hoped to leave a message, and wanted to get off the phone.

"There's a handwritten notation on one of the diaries that says 'Throw these away'. Where did you find these diaries? In the trash?"

"They were . . ." Elias had not anticipated being asked this question, had merely expected that the uncovering of the diaries would be hailed as a glimpse into the Nazi mind. He really should have taken the time to figure out what those handwritten notations meant, and who had written them. "They were in a library."

"Yes, well, be that as it may," Skifford said, his voice heavy with skepticism. "We thank you for your submission. I'm sorry."

The phone went dead. Elias looked down into the grave, where Dixon lay face down, his back glistening with motor oil in the moonlight. He tossed his cellphone to the ground and it clinked off one of the wine bottles.

He tossed another shovelful of dirt into the grave. No thank you – hardly illuminating. The truth was they just didn't have any balls. What did they write about when they did anything on the Second World War? Fucking Normandy. Like that was the only battle. Millions of people fought that war, there were dozens of different governments, each with its own point of view. Wasn't it illuminating to present the point of view of people who lived during the war?

Guess not. Guess history really was written by the winners. The losers didn't even get a mention. Now he'd have to start on something else. Maybe something to do with crime. He had learned a little bit about it lately. Crime. What could he do on crime? Was there a lot of crime in Germany between the wars? Other than the obvious ones, committed by Hitler and the Brownshirts?

Who'd want to read about that? What kind of attention would that get him? Unless, of course, he admitted that he himself had killed someone. Or pretended that he'd robbed a bank. Maybe he could do an article, leave the country and disappear, then admit there was a body in his backyard. That would get him noticed.

He pitched more dirt into the hole, which was almost full now. He felt energy returning.

Crime. He could definitely do a piece about that. The criminal mind.

The possibilities were endless. He loved being an educator.

13

Denise put the coffee on the corner of her desk and stared at her blank computer screen. She had to have a report about the whole Tiburn investigation, or lack of it, on Carver's desk by lunchtime, and she couldn't think of anything to say.

The report only had to be a page of step-by-step on what she and Kohl had done when they were there, but Denise was drawing a blank. The vague sense of discomfort about her Tiburn experience was enveloping her mind, and now she could not form specific images and details, as if she was trying to block them out. Something was wrong. She never had trouble writing reports.

Dick Yancey stuck his head into her cube. "Hey, sweetie. We got a Monday morning meeting in five."

"Shit. I forgot about that." She put her head in her hands.

"You all right?"

"Yeah." She sighed. "Damned Monday meetings." A year ago, Mondays had virtually been a paid day off, but now that so many banks were open on Saturdays, and some even on Sundays, there were always three or four new cases to assign. "Let's go, or we'll get the window seats."

"You sure you're all right?"

"I'm fine, Dick." She tried a warm smile. "Thanks for asking."

Every seat in the conference room was already taken except the two seats by the window, which required a minute or two of everyone else shifting around to even reach.

"Nice of you two to join us," Agent Carver said after the shifting was finished and Dick and Denise were seated. It was two or three minutes before the meeting was scheduled to start and Denise had noticed that upon her entrance, Carver, Walker and Toney had been talking about golf. She was too distracted this morning to bother fighting back with one of her usual underhanded comments, so she just opened her file and looked at them expectantly, saying nothing.

"How was your vacation, Denise?" Carver asked. It was not a polite question. Kohl was sitting next to Carver, and had obviously expressed his concern to the squad supervisor about why Denise had wanted to stay up there.

"It wasn't a vacation," she said, trying to keep hostility from her voice, looking down. "I stayed an extra day because I liked the town."

Carver nodded, then opened his file. Denise figured that even he could sense that she seemed a little darker than usual today, and though he probably attributed it to women's troubles, or some such shit, he knew better than to pursue anything with her.

"Busy weekend," Carver said, now speaking to everyone in the room. "We'll do it in order of amounts taken. A bank manager in Elizabeth, New Jersey, has disappeared, along with three million. Locals found blood in the vault. Doesn't look good for that fellow."

Carver rambled on, and Denise found herself drifting, alert only to the sound of her name. The First Something or Other Bank in Elizabeth. The locals figured the perpetrators had entered the manager's apartment on Saturday night and forced him to drive to the bank and open the vault. They had then emptied . . .

"Apartment?" asked Denise.

Carver stopped reading the file and looked up. "What?"

"He's a bank manager. He lives in an apartment? Why not a house?"

Toney snickered. Carver put the file down and looked at her. "It doesn't mention that in the locals' report, Denise."

"Presumably his bank offers house loans, right? Didn't he qualify for a housing loan at his own bank? How many bank managers live in apartments?"

"This is not an uncommon form of bank robbery," Carver said. "We see these once or twice a year. What are you saying?"

"Usually, when we see them, it's the bank manager's whole family kidnapped at his *house*." She said the last word with emphasis. "I'm saying this guy is single and he lives in an apartment. That would make me wonder."

"Maybe he's divorced," said Toney, smirking.

"Then his ex-wife would be the first person I'd look at," said Denise.

Carver shrugged, turned to Toney. "Agent Toney," he said, sliding him the file. "You take this. And I want the bank manager to be your first choice. I want you to find out about the blood. I want a DNA match to determine whether the blood belongs to the bank manager, and I want to know how much of it there was and where it was found. Until you find something indicating otherwise, I want this treated as an embezzlement." Carver opened the second file. "Portland, Maine," he said.

That was satisfying, at least. Carver wasn't a complete dick all the time. Denise tried to pay attention, but drifted off again, the vague sense of unease returning. It was starting to focus in her mind into something tangible. Bank this, bank that, she heard Carver say. Banks banks banks. Bank robber. I wanted to ask you about the bank robber, Elias had said, when she had been driving back, trying to forget her one-night stand. I wanted to ask you about the bank robber. How's the investigation going?

Elias knew he was a bank robber . . . and she had never once mentioned it to him.

"Oh, Jesus," said Denise aloud, feeling the hairs on her skin stand up as a chill went through her. Elias had known Dixon was a bank robber and she had never told him. She had shown him a picture of Dixon and asked about the missing nurse, and yet he had known Dixon was a bank robber. And he had been talking about banks all during dinner, about where they got their money. And he had been flashing hundred dollar bills, had even given her a hundred dollar bill to HOLD IN HER HAND AND LOOK AT. That must have been one of the bills from the robbery. Oh Jesus. Oh, Christ.

And she had slept with him.

Everyone in the conference room was looking at her, and she became aware she was emitting a low groaning noise. She heard Carver ask if she was all right, but she was already standing and pushing and shoving people out the way to get to the door as a wave of nausea hit her, and she squeezed past Carver, pushing his ample gut into the table with enough force to make him gasp as she opened the conference room door and ran down the hall to the women's room. She slammed the heavy pressed wood door open, and thanked God that both stalls were empty, no secretaries in here fixing their make-up. Just her and the plumbing.

Alone, she felt the nausea ebbing away, being replaced by anger at herself. She had allowed herself to be taken, violated. Elias must have planned it from the beginning, must have imagined a one-night stand with her from the moment they met. He had even asked about Dixon, mentioning that he knew about the bank robbery, as a hint to let her know how smart he was.

Of course, there was nothing she could do now. If she sent the locals to arrest him, the first words out his mouth would be that he had slept with the FBI agent sent to investigate the robbery. She could imagine the jokes already. "There's a guy who's harboring a fugitive in Queens," Carver would say at the conference table, introducing some future investigation. "Let's send Denise out to fuck him." They would slam their coffee mugs on the table in riotous enjoyment of the joke. Her credibility would be ruined.

She leaned over the sink and splashed cool water in her face, dried herself with a paper towel. When she went back into the conference room, there would be concern and questions. She had to have an answer ready. *Something I had for breakfast. That'd do.* She wasn't going to make it easier for them by saying woman troubles.

Jenny Hingston pulled up a chair in Elias's cramped office, putting the first draft of her term paper on the corner of the table and leaning over as if studying it, letting Elias catch a whiff of her perfume. She looked at him expectantly.

"So did you and Miss Police Officer have a nice time after you left?"

Elias nodded. "We did," he said, aware that, to Jenny, his leaving with Denise had increased his value rather than diminished it. "How's the paper coming along?"

Jenny shrugged. "Almost finished," she said, and in a rare moment of honesty, she added, "I'm really sick of this."

"Of what?"

"Of school. I've got two weeks left before I graduate. It's like . . . I feel like I've already graduated, you know? I don't want to do anymore work." She giggled, and stared at him.

"What are you doing over the summer?" Elias asked.

Jenny shrugged again, as if bored. "I dunno. Going back to Concord. Watch TV, go to the gym. What are you doing?"

"I don't know yet," he said. "I was thinking about going to the Bahamas. Just flying down there for a week or two." Oh yes, and perhaps opening an offshore bank account, and dumping $241,300 in a Bahamian safe deposit box.

"Oh, that sounds like fun," Jenny said wistfully. "Are you going by yourself?"

"I dunno." Elias picked up Jenny's term paper and looked at it, flipped through the pages. It was four pages long so far, six fewer than the minimum requirement.

He read a few paragraphs while she waited. The topic was the collapse of the post World War One German economy, and Jenny had taken the one fact she had retained from class – that the German currency had become so devalued in the late 1920s that the people had been reduced to buying ordinary household items with wheelbarrows full of money – and more or less repeated it for four pages. Every paragraph Elias skimmed contained a reference to a wheelbarrow.

He put the paper down. "I'd like to take someone," he said. "But I can't take a student. It would be against the rules."

"I'm not going to be a student anymore in two weeks," she said breathily.

Elias nodded, and handed the paper back to her. "You don't need to do anymore work on that," he said. "It looks fine just the way it is."

Melissa Covington walked out of Willard's Coffee Shop with her best friend Emily, having spent eight of the ten dollars her father had given her that morning for her weekly lunch allowance on two chocolate milkshakes, which had been marketed as frozen fudge mocha cappuccinos.

"You've got to see them, they are so cute," Melissa said. She was returning to an argument they had been having all day, trying to get Emily to come over to see her cat's new litter of kittens. Emily wanted to, but protested that she had to return home to babysit her younger brother.

"How about tomorrow?" Emily asked. "Tomorrow I could actually stay for a while. My little retard of a brother has baseball practice . . ."

But Melissa wasn't listening. She had stopped walking, and was staring, as if frozen, her drink held to her lips. Emily, who had been walking just behind, almost bumped into her.

"Shit, I almost spilled this all over your back. What're you looking at?"

"Ohmigod, I know this guy," Melissa said, grabbing Emily's arm. She pointed at the wanted poster on the bulletin board directly outside the police station. "He was at my neighbor's house yesterday."

"Oh, bullshit," said Emily.

"No, really, I swear. I was talking to him. I showed him one of the kittens." Melissa read the poster. Wanted for Armed Robbery. Philip Turner Dixon. "That's him," she said, her voice rising with excitement. "His name was Phil."

"You're on crack," said Emily, but she was getting excited, too. They read the poster together. "Ohmigod, he's like, armed and dangerous. He could have killed you."

"He seemed like a nice guy," Melissa said. "He liked the kitten."

"He's armed and dangerous and he likes kittens," said Emily, and they both giggled. "Where did you see him?"

"He was at Elias's house. Sitting on the back porch."

"Oh, Elias," Emily said. "It's Elias now, is it."

"Shut *up*," Melissa squealed. "He's just my neighbor."

"Whatever. You hooked up with him, didn't you?"

"He got me drunk," said Melissa, and they both giggled.

"Whatever."

"Whatever yourself."

"That's not him," said Emily definitively, looking at the picture. "It can't be him. No one like that comes here."

"Nah, it's probably not him," Melissa agreed. "This guy's from Texas. The guy I met was from Kentucky." She stared at the poster for a few more seconds. "It really looks like him, though."

"You're on crack," said Emily again.

Melissa's attention was drawn to the movement in the building next door to the police station, where a guy working in The Tiburn Bakery was putting a fresh sheet of chocolate chip cookies in the display case.

"Ohmigod," she said, as if she had just solved a mystery. She grabbed Emily's arm. "Let's get some cookies."

"COOOOKIES," Emily growled, doing her best impression of the Cookie Monster.

They both burst into giggles and ran off into the bakery.

Epilogue

Elias was practicing his speech at his desk when Alice came in. He didn't like the speech at all; he thought it was boring, nothing like one he would have written himself. It was all about testing water tables and improving air quality and finding funding for a local pumping station, all of which he was promising to do. He would rather be talking about intangibles, like hope and dreams, things for which he could not be held accountable if they failed to materialize. And if you talked about hope and dreams, you could talk like Martin Luther King and get a reputation as a great orator, which, deep down, Elias knew he was. He doubted very much that children would be reciting King's speeches decades later if The Dream had been to decrease property taxes by six percent over the next three years.

Elias's entry into politics had come as a direct result of his relationship with Jenny Hingston, whose father ran a luxury auto dealership in Concord. Prior to taking her to the Caribbean, Jenny had insisted on introducing him to her parents, despite Elias's unease, and Geoff Hingston had been instantly taken with the idea of entering Elias into a political race. It turned out that when not selling overpriced vehicles, Geoff Hingston spent his time in the governor's office, selecting candidates for the state senate. Elias's youthful appearance, his charisma, and his learned and stable background would appeal to New Hampshire voters, Hingston insisted. Elias made him insist because he liked hearing it, all the while knowing that this, rather than teaching, was his true calling. As for being a thirty-five-year-old college professor who was sleeping with his twenty-one-year-old daughter, Geoff Hingston didn't seem fazed one bit.

State senate. Young as he was, he could do two or three terms before moving up to national politics. How long was a state senate term, anyway? He would need to find out. In the meantime, he had to learn about water tables. What the fuck was an aquifer, anyway? Didn't water come from streams? Why was half his speech about water? He would need to bring it up with his handlers, and he wasn't entirely sure that they knew what they were doing. He didn't want to start out his political career boring people to death.

Alice saw that he was working and quietly slid the mail on his desk, then closed the door softly. He nodded thanks to her as he looked at the mail, glad for the distraction. On top of a pile of the usual crap was a large manila envelope from a prominent university in California. Hmmmm. Elias picked it up and examined it. Could they have heard about his Nazism article? Did they want to publish it? In California? Doubtful. It wasn't going to happen now, anyway. That was the type of thing that could ruin a political career. After talking with a number of people at scholarly publications, Elias had decided that his article had just been too explosive, too raw, for the establishment to handle, and after talking with Jenny Hingston's dad, had figured it was just the type of thing that needed to be buried forever if he was to have any type of career in politics. Still, it was nice to get a call back.

He opened the envelope and realized right away that it was not about the article. It was a stack of forms with a cover letter.

Dear Professor White:

We are pleased to inform you that you have been selected as a referee by an applicant for a teaching position at our university. As we have a highly selective screening process, we would appreciate your taking the utmost care in filling out the enclosed papers, and returning them to this address by March 31. Thank you in advance for your time and consideration,

Sincerely,

Dean Evelyn Wister

Elias stared at it, confused. Who the hell was citing him as a referee? You would think a recommendation for one of his students might be a little more heartfelt if he knew who they were. He flipped the cover letter and looked at the forms beneath, and saw the name in small point type at the top of the first page: reference list for Denise Lupo.

Denise Lupo. Well I'll be damned. The FBI girl. She was applying for a teaching job and had picked him as her academic reference.

He wondered what to do about it. What could he honestly say in a reference? That she was good in bed? He doubted that was the information the university was after. He put the reference papers on the desk and looked at his other mail. Some letters from concerned parents, something from the local chapter of the Police Athletic League (he was a regular contributor) and, at the bottom of the pile, a letter with an FBI motif with a New York City postmark. Oh boy.

He opened the FBI letter. It was, as he suspected, from Denise. It was typed and very official-looking, no perfume.

Dear Professor White

I wanted to thank you for your hospitality during my stay in Tiburn. As it turns out, I have applied to a number of colleges for teaching positions and have listed you as a referee. Please make sure to mention that we have known each other for over two years.

I think it's been about that long, hasn't it? I lose track
of time.

Thanks so much,

Agent Denise Lupo

Two years, Elias thought. The whole episode had been
barely five months ago. At the bottom were two other
notes, also typed.

PS We never did find that bank robber, but I have a
very strong theory about where he is. Oh well. As soon
as I get a teaching job, it will all just be water under
the bridge.

PPS. Please do try to get the references finished by
March 31. Thanks so much.

And a smiley face. She had drawn a fucking smiley face.
Elias shook his head as he tossed the letter onto the
desk.

A very strong theory about where he is . . .

He looked at the reference forms again. It wouldn't
be so bad. An hour or two at most, he could write a
reference that would get Denise a teaching job at any
Ivy League school in the country.

There was a knock on the door and Jenny Hingston
came in without waiting for a response. Alice never

stopped her anymore. She was a graduate student now, on her way to a master's in history, and Elias was, of course, her personal advisor. Alice was no fool.

"Ready for lunch?" she asked.

"Ready. Let me get my coat."

Elias got up and looked at the reference forms again. That would be fine. He would get her a nice teaching job somewhere, and everyone would be happy. What a great country we live in, he thought.

Everything has worked out well for everybody.